Straight-A
Teacher

Books by Beverly Lewis

GIRLS ONLY (GO!)
Youth Fiction

Dreams on Ice	*Follow the Dream*
Only the Best	*Better Than Best*
A Perfect Match	*Photo Perfect*
Reach for the Stars	*Star Status*

SUMMERHILL SECRETS
Youth Fiction

Whispers Down the Lane	*House of Secrets*
Secret in the Willows	*Echoes in the Wind*
Catch a Falling Star	*Hide Behind the Moon*
Night of the Fireflies	*Windows on the Hill*
A Cry in the Dark	*Shadows Beyond the Gate*

HOLLY'S HEART
Youth Fiction

Best Friend, Worst Enemy	*California Crazy*
Secret Summer Dreams	*Second-Best Friend*
Sealed With a Kiss	*Good-Bye, Dressel Hills*
The Trouble With Weddings	*Straight-A Teacher*

www.BeverlyLewis.com

Straight-A
Teacher

Beverly Lewis

BETHANYHOUSE
Minneapolis, Minnesota

Straight-A Teacher
Copyright © 2002
Beverly Lewis

Cover illustration by Paul Casale
Cover design by Cheryl Neisen

Published by Bethany House Publishers
A Ministry of Bethany Fellowship International
11400 Hampshire Avenue South
Bloomington, Minnesota 55438
www.bethanyhouse.com

Printed in the United States of America by
Bethany Press International, Bloomington, Minnesota 55438

Library of Congress Cataloging-in-Publication Data

Lewis, Beverly, 1949-
    Straight-A teacher / by Beverly Lewis.
        p.   cm. — (Holly's heart ; 8)
Summary: Fourteen-year-old Holly develops a crush on Mr. Barnett, the new student teacher in drama class.
    ISBN 0-7642-2615-0
    [1. Friendship—Fiction. 2. Student teachers—Fiction. 3. Teachers—Fiction. 4. Schools—Fiction. 5. Musicals—Fiction. 6. Christian life—Fiction.] I. Title.
    PZ7.L58464 Sde   2002
    [Fic]—dc21   2002010725

Author's Note

Thanks to all who have helped make the HOLLY'S HEART series a successful reality: the editorial team at Bethany House Publishers, my SCBWI group, Barbara Birch, and my husband, Dave Lewis.

As always, I can count on my kid consultants: Kirsten, Julie, Amy, Shanna, Mindie, Aleya, Kristin, Anastasia, Jonathan, and Janie for fantastic ideas and input. Hugs to each of you!

Special thanks to Bob Billingsley for his knowledge of the classic Thunderbird sports car.

For my dear readers,
especially those who share
heart secrets with me.

I was late for fourth-period choir. Really late. Today Miss Hess, our choral director, was auditioning students for the lead role of Maria in *The Sound of Music*. And I was competing against all my girl friends for the part.

Holding on to my notebook, I heaved the rest of my books into my locker and slammed the door. Then I dashed down the hall, past the principal's office, and spun around the corner.

Whoosh! I plowed into someone. My notebook flew out of my hands, creating a fan of loose papers all over the floor.

"I'm sorry," I gasped, looking up. And there he was: the cutest guy I had ever seen. Soft gray eyes. A flash of a dimple in his smile. And just a hint of a five-o'clock shadow.

"Are you all right?" His gentle voice took my breath away.

I mumbled a pathetic apology. "I'm really s-sorry." Stuttering wasn't my style, but this guy . . . My heart flipped and fluttered like some poor, unsuspecting fish dragged up on the sand.

"Are you sure you're all right?" he asked again, this time touching my arm. The warmth of his touch came through my sweater, toasting my elbow.

I managed a nod.

"It was my fault," he insisted, leaning over to gather up my papers.

Slightly dazed, I reached for my notebook. It was then I noticed the navy blue sleeve of his sweater and his nicely pressed khakis. This guy was too young to be a parent, he was certainly not a teacher, and he was too old for junior high. In fact, I'd never seen him around Dressel Hills before.

Slowly standing, he handed the pile of papers to me, glancing at the one on top. "Holly Meredith," he remarked as he studied it. "Are you a teacher's assistant?" His eyes twinkled as he spoke.

Delightfully surprised, I shook my head slowly. At once his eyes met mine, and for an instant, I felt the planet shift on its axis.

"I'd better hurry," I heard myself say. With a fleeting smile, I scurried off to the stairway and up to the music room.

As I pushed open the choir room door, Miss Hess stood behind a music stand, organizing her music folder. She wore a long denim skirt and plaid western shirt. More fashion conscious than the older teachers, Miss Hess had a wardrobe that just wouldn't quit.

Jared grinned at me from the tenor section, and Andie and Paula motioned for me to sit between them in the soprano section. I hurried to take my seat.

"You're late," Andie whispered. It wasn't just a statement; she wanted details.

I fidgeted, not ready to divulge my glorious encounter with the sweater-and-pressed-khakis guy. Just how old was he, anyway? I called up his face in my imagination. The hint of a beard and the way he dressed told me he was in his late teens—or early twenties. I still couldn't believe he'd actually mistaken me for a grown woman!

Andie jabbed me in the ribs. "Snap to it, Meredith," she whispered.

Still giddy, I tried to pay attention as Miss Hess gave instructions for the tryouts. "To cut down on after-school time, we're having auditions during class," she began. "*The Sound of Music* is a classic, as all of you probably know. The roles of Maria and Captain von Trapp will involve major commitment on the part of the girl and guy who win the leads this year." She paused, studying the competition perched on the risers around us.

Commitment? Dedication? Shoot, I'd ingest frog legs for the part of Maria! But then, so would Andie on my right and Paula on my left. I sighed.

Behind us, little sevies sat in clusters of four or more, exchanging nervous whispers and frantic looks, while we sophisticated female students of Dressel Hills Junior High—eighth graders, of course—sat poised and calm. As always, there were a few top-of-the-heap ninth graders acting disgustingly pert and casually cool as usual on the back row of the risers—the Pinnacle of Pride. The truly cool ninth graders, like Danny Myers and my friends Paula and Kayla Miller, sat closer to the front.

Miss Hess began to hand out copies of the script, a stack to each row. Danny Myers offered to help her. When he passed my row, he made a point to catch my eye. "Break a leg, Holly," he said. The twinkle in his eye was hard to ignore. That was Danny, a super-serious Christian and a very encouraging guy.

I returned his smile. "Thanks. You too." But secretly, my heart sank. What if he *did* get the part of Captain von Trapp? And what if I was Maria? Yikes! We'd have to act like we were in love. *That would add fuel to the fire*, I thought, remembering what Andie had said last week. She thought Danny still liked me. We'd had our chance at romance last summer. I'd actually fallen for a redhead. Well . . . auburn, really. Now Danny and I were merely good friends. End of story.

Andie poked me again. "Who's that?" she whispered, staring at a tall, good-looking guy conferring with Miss Hess across the room.

At first, it didn't register who he was, but then the sweater triggered my memory. I jerked to attention as Miss Hess introduced him.

"Class, I'd like you to meet my student teacher. Mr. Barnett will assist me as drama coach throughout the remaining weeks of the semester," she explained. "We are truly fortunate to have this talented young man on board."

The student teacher smiled as we applauded. "Thanks," he said, glancing around the room. "I'm looking forward to working with each of you to make this the best performance ever." With that, he picked up his notebook and sat on the risers with the tenors, like one of the guys.

My heart thumped as I watched him pull a pen out of his shirt pocket, underneath his sweater. His hands moved with such purpose. Like a seasoned professor of drama, he was poised to eliminate the competition, narrowing us down to the choice few. Mr. Barnett clicked his pen, and unexpectedly, he turned and caught my stare. Embarrassed, I looked down at the script portion in my lap. If I was to try out for Maria, I'd better focus on things at hand. But Mr. Barnett's face was before me, clouding my senses. This audition would be tricky.

After giving us several minutes to study scripts, Miss Hess asked for volunteers to read parts.

Amy-Liz, a spunky, curly-haired soprano, raised her hand. Mr. Barnett met her alongside the piano. He leaned on the console piano and briefly discussed the scene. Then Amy-Liz stood tall and began the scene without ever referring to the script!

But an even bigger surprise followed. Mr. Barnett began playing the part of Captain von Trapp. It was a romantic scene, where he tells Maria he loves her.

Miss Hess stopped the scene, encouraging Amy-Liz to act more romantic. *So that's what she wants*, I thought, carefully scanning the script. A super-romantic female lead? I fidgeted as the scene progressed.

"I can pour on the mushy stuff if that's what it takes," Andie whispered in my ear.

I really wanted to tell her: *Please mess up!* But all I said was, "Better be careful, Stan's watching." Stan, my sixteen-year-old cousin-turned-stepbrother, was her longest-running boyfriend ever.

Soon it was Andie's turn. She hardly waited for Amy-Liz to sit down before she started. She was doing fine until she totally blew it by giggling halfway through the scene. It was the most immature thing imaginable!

By the end of the hour, most of my friends had auditioned for the part of Maria, including Paula Miller and her twin, Kayla. Jared Wilkins, my former guy friend, kept staring at me from the opposite side of the risers, trying to get me to try out next. Even though the romance was officially over between us, he still liked to flirt with me a little.

Danny watched me, too. Was he worried I'd get the part, opposite some other guy? He kept crossing his legs, first the right, then the left. It was obvious he was restless. Maybe he wasn't so sure about watching me audition the part. Of course, there would be no real romantic stuff, just the script . . . at least for today.

"Well, are you gonna audition or not?" Andie asked.

I could tell by the gleam in her eye that she hoped I'd back out.

"Of course!" I answered, thinking Andie would make a better von Trapp *kid* than Maria.

Miss Hess called my name. "Hurry, Holly," she said glancing at the clock. "We have time for one more."

It should be easy now, after observing so many girls audition the part. I made my way down the risers, feeling comfortable with the text and the action. . . .

But there was Mr. Barnett's face again. His gentle eyes seemed to search out mine, of all the possible Marias in the room. It was as though he could see me, look through the layers of me . . . into the real Holly Meredith. The mature me, the me that had begun to emerge.

Breathing deeply, I began.

2

From the moment I opened my mouth to speak, it was as though Mr. Barnett and I were alone in the room. Alone, except for the rhythmic interplay of dialogue and drama. Effortlessly, I blocked out the observers. The two of us, Mr. Barnett and I, soon became the actual characters we portrayed. He, the older, the Captain Georg von Trapp, and I, the younger, the innocent Maria. When he said his lines, his face seemed to light up.

The applause startled me as the scene came to an end. "Encore!" I heard Jared yelling.

"Go, Meredith!" Stan hollered.

Sad that it had to end, I relished the applause.

We were fabulous together, Mr. Barnett and I. Too bad he wasn't a student, I thought. But then the rich maturity he possessed would be missing. That thought settled over me as the clapping swelled to a gentle roar, careful not to expose my true emotions as I returned to my seat between Andie and Paula.

Paula made a circle with her thumb and pointer finger. "Par excellence," she said. But her weak smile gave her away. I knew how badly she wanted the part.

Andie grabbed my arm, a bit harder than usual. "Hey, you missed the giggling part!" she teased. I could tell she was afraid she'd blown it with her laughter.

"Yeah, right." I pulled away from her viselike grip.

Danny's serious gaze caught my eye as I glanced at the tenor section. What was *he* thinking?

Miss Hess grinned from her desk. "A stunning performance," she said, looking first at Mr. Barnett, then at me. Had she forgotten the other prospective Marias in the room? Quickly, she composed herself and announced, "We've had many wonderful Marias today. And Mr. Barnett and I will post the winner on Friday. Tomorrow, we'll be on the lookout for our best Captain. Get ready, guys!"

Jared raised his hand. "Who's playing Maria for *our* auditions?"

"You're looking at her." Miss Hess curtsied comically.

I felt someone tap my shoulder and turned to see a folded note on the floor behind me. I picked it up and read it.

Dear Holly,
    Will you sit with me at youth group this Thursday? I'll call you soon.
                                Very sincerely,
                                Danny

Andie wasn't kidding! Danny *was* interested. No wonder he'd watched my every move today. No wonder he seemed to have a tough time while I pretended to be in love with Mr. Barnett. *Pretended?*

"Better watch out," Andie whispered, eyeing the note. "Next thing you know, you'll have Danny Myers running your life again."

"Fat chance." I stuffed the note into my pocket and grabbed my notebook just as the bell rang. Hurrying to my locker, with Andie at my side, I replayed the audition in my mind. I was totally overwhelmed with Mr. Barnett.

♥   ♥   ♥

After school, at home, I trembled as I wrote in my journal. *Monday, April 11: What a fabulous day! Today was the beginning of something incredible and new. Mr. Barnett is our gorgeous student drama teacher for Miss Hess. I ran into him in the hall on the way to choir. And then he auditioned with me when I tried out for the part of Maria. From the moment we met, he seemed to notice something in me—something I'm only now beginning to recognize in myself. Maturity!*

I put my pen down and read my journal entry, just thinking. And then it came to me—the perfect way to get to know Mr. Barnett better. Why hadn't I thought of this before? I would interview him for the school paper. Fabulous idea!

Writing for *The Lift* was something new for me. I had just seen my first article in print—a light-hearted interview with the cafeteria cook. It had taken lots of work, including the actual interview, the rough draft, and the rewriting—three or four times. But for Mr. Barnett, I was more than willing to put in the required additional work.

I picked up my pen and twirled it between my fingers, reliving the collision in the hall, how his eyes met mine, the warmth of his hand on my elbow. . . . In the midst of giggling, game-playing junior high girls, Mr. Barnett had encountered a mature soul. Mine.

Thoughts of Danny crept into my head. Could I handle him in a diplomatic fashion? I didn't want to hurt him. Not again.

It all came rushing back. Last summer, Danny and I had been good buddies. He'd even rescued me from that horrid-smelling outhouse at the top of Copper Mountain! But it had taken all summer for him to finally ask me out. After I said yes, things coasted along fine between us at first, but soon he was trying to run my life. With the Bible, no less!

It was a nightmare. And finally I had called it quits by storming out of the Soda Straw during a church ice-cream social. Danny had been humiliated, and I felt lousy. Eventually, we worked things out between us so we could be friends again—just the way we were now. The way we were going to stay.

I went to the hall phone and called him. He answered on the first ring. *Too eager,* I thought.

"Hi, Danny," I said. "Got your note."

"That's good." He sounded nervous, really nervous.

"You know, we've discussed all this before," I began.

"I know, still—"

I interrupted him. "It won't work, Danny. You're one of my best friends. Can't we just keep it that way?"

I could hear him breathing. Sort of. "You okay?" I asked, feeling sad for him.

"Sure, Holly, I'm fine. But think about it, okay?"

I hated being so hard on him. For one thing, I knew it had taken loads of courage to send this note. For another thing, he was a year older, and I wanted to look up to him, to respect him. But his pleading like this bugged me.

Sounding a bit dejected, Danny hung up. Hopefully the boy-girl issue was behind us now.

I sat down and pondered the selection of male students and made a decision. "Boys my age are a waste of time," I said to myself.

♥　♥　♥

Tuesday after school, I stopped off to see Marcia Green, the student editor of *The Lift*. Peeking over her long desk, I noticed a few of the memos she'd written. My name appeared several times on yellow stickies posted on the wall near her desk. By the looks of things, she had other article ideas for me to pursue.

Marcia looked up from the manuscripts she was proofreading. "Hey, Holly. What's up?"

That's when I volunteered to interview Mr. Barnett for the April issue of *The Lift*.

"Great idea." Marcia picked up her pen and tapped it on the desk. "Thanks for the suggestion." I turned to leave, but she continued, "Stop by Thursday after lunch, Holly. I'll have some preliminary stuff for you on Mr. Barnett."

"Okay, thanks," I said.

She nodded, already preoccupied with her work, completely oblivious to the gravity of my situation. Mine and Mr. Barnett's.

At lunch on Wednesday, talk of the leading roles for the school musical buzzed everywhere. In hot-lunch line, at the tables . . . It hovered in the air. The guys were split on their personal choices for Maria. It appeared to be a close contest between Amy-Liz . . . and me. But Miss Hess was notorious for being unpredictable. At this stage, it was anyone's guess who'd be chosen for the female lead.

I sat in the cafeteria with Paula and Andie, at our usual spot next to the windows. Settling down with a bowl of chili smothered in cheese, I gazed out the window. Time and place disappeared as I daydreamed, staring at the mountains, the new foliage. Spring was here. New beginnings. . . .

"Holly, you're doing it again," Andie's voice careened into my private thoughts.

"What?" I turned away from the window and dipped my spoon into the cheesy chili.

"You know what." She sounded exasperated.

"It's called daydreaming," Paula intervened. "Pure and simple, and there's no crime in it." She flashed her million-dollar smile.

"Thanks for your insight, Paula," I laughed.

"So . . . what's on your mind?" Andie was pushing.

I ignored her, sipping some milk.

"Oh, let me guess," Andie said. "You're dying for the part of Maria, right?"

It would've been so easy to agree with her, just

to get her off my back. In fact, landing the role of Maria took only second place to what was really on my mind. The way I figured it, the girl getting the part of Maria would have the most personal contact with Mr. Barnett.

"Maybe it's a secret," Paula offered, defending my right to privacy once again.

Andie snorted. "Could be, but if it is, Holly always breaks down and tells all. That's how she is." Her dark eyes danced with mischief.

It felt weird hearing her discuss my faults right under my nose. She kept it up. "First, Holly's crazy over Jared Wilkins, then she likes Danny Myers, and then she dumps Danny and goes marching back to Jared. You never know what to expect from this girl!" Andie's words pierced my heart.

Paula studied me with sympathetic eyes. She actually looked prettier these days without the inch-thick mascara. Thanks to an afternoon spent at Holly's beauty salon.

"At this age, we're changeable," Paula said. "Holly's our friend. That's what counts."

Paula had a point. Maybe it would help Andie to hear someone else's opinion of me for a change.

Quickly, I changed the subject, before Andie had a chance for a comeback. Knowing her, she'd have one eventually. "Who do you think will get Captain von Trapp?" I asked.

Paula spoke up. "Danny's taller than most of the

ninth-grade boys, but he can't act."

"He can memorize fast," I commented. "But you're right, Jared's the better actor and singer."

Andie chimed in. "I could see Jared and Amy-Liz onstage together."

"How can you *say* that?" I shot back. What a low blow! And from my best friend!

"Well, what do you want to hear?" she said. "I'd give anything to put myself in Maria's shoes—next to Jared's. How's that?"

I shook my head, not letting her get to me with her dumb remarks. "Let's just see who Miss Hess and Mr. Barnett pick for the part, okay?"

"Miss Hess seems fair enough, but I don't know about Mr. Barnett," Andie replied. "He's got his teacher's pets picked out already. I noticed it right away."

Gulp! What had Andie noticed?

Paula pulled on her brunette locks. "I don't think Mr. Barnett plays favorites. He's just super nice."

"Maybe you're right," Andie said without looking at me. She pushed her chair out and went to get more soda.

When Andie was out of earshot, Paula asked, "Do *you* think Mr. Barnett has favorites?"

I shrugged my shoulders, pretending not to care.

Jared came over and sat down. I breathed a sigh of relief as the conversation made a complete turn. Away from Mr. Barnett.

Thursday during choir, I did my best to avoid eye contact with Mr. Barnett. He sat on Miss Hess's desk, arms folded across his ribbed burgundy sweater, waiting for everyone to arrive.

Restless chatter filled the room as students, eager for tryouts, jostled and hooted back and forth. Today, auditions were being held for the abbey nuns, Sister Berthe and Sister Sophia, Franz the butler, and some of the older von Trapp children. I blocked out the noise, imagining my upcoming interview with Mr. Barnett. I, with my notebook and pen, poised to ask thoughtful, intelligent questions. And he, responding in gentle yet cautious tones. Just the two of us.

"Earth to Holly," Andie whispered.

I jumped. "Huh?"

"You look dazed, girl," she said. "I think we better have a talk."

My cheeks grew warm as the lingering vision slowly faded. "About what?"

Andie's finger poked my enflamed cheek. "About that."

The din of chatter subsided as Mr. Barnett stood, notebook in hand. He cleared his throat. "Okay, students. This is home stretch." Here, he scanned the room with his eyes. Once again they found mine, if only for an instant.

Heart thudding, I wondered how I'd ever find the courage to arrange my interview with him. After all, I would have to speak to him to set it up.

I stared at Miss Hess sitting at the piano. She listened intently as Mr. Barnett made announcements. Was she grading him mentally? Isn't that what supervising teachers had to do—grade their student teachers based on performance and progress? I couldn't imagine Mr. Barnett getting less than straight A's.

The pink floral pattern in Miss Hess's below-the-knee skirt caught my attention. I stared at the shimmery oranges and swirling pinks. What was it like, spending each school day, every day, from now until the end of school with someone like Mr. Barnett? I envied Miss Hess.

After class, I took my sweet time gathering my things, hoping the classroom would clear out in a hurry. I didn't want Paula or Andie to know about the interview I was planning. So far, at least, my secret was safe.

"Hurry, Holly," Andie called over her shoulder, rushing for the door with Paula. "We'll save you a seat at lunch."

Lunch or not, I had to talk to Mr. Barnett about the interview. But now Danny was in my way—discussing props and stage management with him. Glancing over at the piano, I noticed that Miss Hess had already left for lunch, too. Fabulous timing! Now if only I could get Danny to disappear.

Eavesdropping on Danny's conversation with Mr. Barnett made me jittery. I shuffled my feet and self-consciously watched the clock on the wall. Its second hand jerked rhythmically, reminding me of how little time I had left for lunch.

Shifting my books, I gave up and headed out the door.

Danny caught up to me in the hall. "Holly, I'm finished," he said. "Thanks for waiting around."

Oh no, I thought. *He thinks I waited for him!*

"Can we eat together?" He followed me down the hall to my locker.

"I, uh . . . Andie and Paula . . . I think . . . are saving me a place."

"I don't mind sitting with your friends. If it's okay with you."

Of course it wasn't, but I nodded my consent anyway. It was the only decent thing to do after the way I'd treated him on the phone.

Andie's eyes nearly popped when Danny and I showed up together at lunch. I shot her a warning with my eyes. She caught the secret message—every bit of it. Andie knew better than to make some dumb remark about Danny and me being a couple again.

We spent most of lunch discussing Mr. Barnett. Danny got it going. "What do you think of our new student teacher?"

"He knows theater, that's for sure," Paula said. "Did you see how he marked off the floor in the music room when Billy auditioned for the butler? I tell you, he's good."

"He wants me to be stage manager," Danny said.

"No fair. You know what you're gonna be before us," Andie teased, pretending to pout.

How childish, I thought, watching Andie mope. But deep inside, I was secretly relieved to know Danny was out of the running for the male lead.

"What do you think of Mr. Barnett?" Andie asked me. She leaned forward on the table, balancing herself on her elbows, her impish eyes flashing. She seemed to suspect something, and I resented her for asking me right in front of everyone. It was another one of her childish, more immature traits.

"Mr. Barnett?" I said casually, willing my pulse to slow. "I agree with Paula. He seems to know his stuff."

"That's it?" Andie said.

Danny stopped eating his spaghetti, which featured chunks of yellow-green mystery meat mixed with off-white worms, er, noodles.

I forced my gaze away from the worms of the week and focused on Danny's eyes, which were so close I could see gold flecks in them. It was as though he—and Paula and Andie—were waiting to pounce on my secret.

"What's there to say?" I responded. "I think Miss Hess should have a student teacher every year for the spring musical." I reached for my napkin.

If my friends only knew...

Danny excused himself from the table. "Nice having lunch with you, Holly." He turned beet red, no doubt realizing he'd eaten with all three of us.

"Any time at all," Andie piped up.

"See you, Danny," Paula said, smiling and waving.

It was a strained moment, all right. But the second Danny was out of sight, we burst out laughing. It wasn't fair to make fun of him, but Danny had it coming. He'd literally set himself up by acting like a love-sick toad.

I hurried off to the girls' rest room to wash my hands and check my makeup and hair. My plan was to intercept Mr. Barnett somehow. I needed to set up the interview with him. Not because I had a pressing editorial deadline, but because it was part of my plan. Besides, I was dying to talk to him. One mature soul to another.

I dried my hands, glancing at my watch. Time was running out! Hurrying into the hall, I scoped out the area for signs of Andie or Paula. Danny too. No way did I want them spying on me.

All clear. I dashed upstairs, heading for the music room. Tiptoeing up to the door, I peeked in the window.

Yes! He was there. Taking a deep breath, I knocked.

"Come in," he called.

Trembling, I turned the doorknob and let myself in.

"Oh, hello there, Holly," he said, looking up from his desk. He remembered my name! I nearly hyperventilated on the spot.

"Is something wrong?" A slight frown played across his brow.

"Oh, nothing's wrong," I said, trying to regain my composure. "I just wanted to talk to you about—"

Suddenly Miss Hess breezed into the room. "Andrew," she called. "I need to see you in the teacher's lounge." A flirtatious smile played across her lips as she turned and left as quickly as she'd come.

Andrew?

"I'm very sorry, Holly," he apologized, standing up. "Can we talk later?"

I wanted to ask when but only nodded, standing there in a daze, watching the most wonderful man in the world disappear through the choir room door.

I sighed. "His name is Andrew," I whispered reverently. In a fog, I stared at his cluttered desk, piled with papers and the open notebook. Suddenly the image of Mr. Barnett's precious notebook leaped out at me. There were students' names listed beside names of characters.

I froze, trying not to entertain the thought of snooping. Yet I was tempted. Tempted with one of my greatest weaknesses.

Think how easy it would be to take one quick look. One secret look. No one will ever have to know. . . .

It was the Garden of Eden all over again—Eve listening to the voice of the tempter. And just like Eve, I inched forward and reached for the forbidden fruit.

I scanned the list. There was Danny Myers as stage manager, Stan Patterson, my stepbrother, as Rolf Gruber. Andie was listed beside Mother Abbess. I could almost hear her singing "Climb Every Mountain." I couldn't picture her, however, as the Reverend Mother of Nonnberg Abbey!

Laughing out loud, I ran my finger halfway down the list, searching for my name.

Br-ring! Br-ring! The fire alarm rang out. Startled, I ran out of the choir room. I couldn't see or smell any evidence of fire or smoke. Quickly, I headed for the nearest exit, slipping in line with other students. I was disappointed about not finding my name. Now I'd have to wait, like everyone else, till tomorrow morning.

Andie fell in line with me outside. "Probably just another silly drill," she said. "We've had twenty-five of them already this year."

"Not even close," I said, wondering why she had to exaggerate like that. Another sign of her lack of maturity.

Suddenly I spotted Mr. Barnett. He was hurrying out of the building with Miss Hess and several other teachers. I watched the way he walked, the way he interacted with them. I watched Miss Hess, too. She seemed quite attentive to Mr. Barnett. Was it her way of being a good supervisory teacher, or was there more to it?

Jared joined us, his voice interrupting my thoughts. "This is some cool way to spend a lunch hour."

"Yeah," Andie said, eyeballing me. "What happened to *you*? One minute you were primping in the rest room, next thing, you were gone." Her eyes twinkled with a zillion questions.

Jared grinned, elbowing my arm. "Sounds like you've got a second mother here."

"I'm her guardian angel," Andie retorted. "She's sneaking around, up to something." She twisted a curl around her finger.

I tried to visualize Andie draped in the robes of the Mother Abbess. I couldn't help myself; I snickered.

"Now what?" she demanded.

"Oh, nothing." I waved my hand, flipping my long ponytail.

"You're hopeless," she said. "But I'll get to the

bottom of this sooner or later." She probably would, too.

Several more minutes passed before the all-clear bell rang and we filed inside. Fifth hour was pending, so we headed like a herd of cattle to the rows of lockers.

After school, I dropped in to see Marcia Green about the interview stuff. I held my breath as she thumbed through her notebook. "Let's see," she muttered to herself. "I know it's here somewhere."

Pulling up a chair, I waited impatiently for Marcia to find my new assignment. I twisted my hair and bit on the ends. Crazy as it seemed, I was actually going to interview Mr. Andrew Barnett!

"Here it is." Marcia held up the file at last. "I'll need good copy by next week." She looked at the calendar. "Next Thursday, a week from today. Think you can squeeze it into your schedule?"

"No problem," I said, caressing the file. The name in black marker leaped off the file at me.

Andrew Barnett.

His name alone made my heart jump. Could I still it long enough to conduct a reasonably intelligent interview? The thought flamed my cheeks. I dashed down the hall, hoping to create a breeze strong enough to fan my flushed face. Had to before Andie saw me and pumped me with questions.

"Holly, wait up!"

It was Andie. But I kept going, blowing air out

my lips. Another couple of seconds and maybe, just maybe, the red would drain from my cheeks. . . .

"Listen, girl, if you don't slow down, you'll attract Coach Tucker's attention for sure," Andie hollered.

She had me.

I turned around. "Miss Tucker better not nab me for track tryouts," I muttered. "I despise running."

"But it's that time of year," Andie sang, "track and field." Then she searched my face. "You're blushing again. *Now* what's going on?"

We'd had this conversation before. "It's nothing, really." No way could I tell her. I shoved Mr. Barnett's file down, out of sight.

We pushed through the crowded hallway. "Holly, you're avoiding me," she said.

"Right." I laughed. "That's impossible."

The sound of slamming lockers and the bustle of scurrying students interrupted my thoughts. When we stopped at Andie's locker, she flicked through her combination and pulled on the door. I hurried to my locker, opened it, and stuffed the file safely behind another notebook just as Andie came over.

Although I was usually perfectly content to be in Andie's company and was comfortable with our ongoing friendship, I was discovering more and more that I didn't want to expose my heart for examination with her like I used to. Andie was developing a high-and-mighty way about her. Evolving, my mother had said. Well, whatever it was, Andie was establishing a know-it-all attitude that made me uneasy.

Stan showed up and Andie beamed at him. They were still going strong after several months. Andie turned to me with that all-too-familiar glint in her eye. "We're off to the Soda Straw, Holly. But I guarantee you'll tell me your little secret, sooner or later." She accented her words with a bang of her locker and a rambunctious wave.

Overconfident. That described Andie, all right. It seemed she was forever rehearsing the part of an outspoken, self-assured woman. Hopefully, by the time she grew up, Andie would learn not to fire shots that pierced the soul of her friends. Maybe she would learn something from the role of Mother Abbess.

I began sorting my books as I analyzed my relationship with Andie. It had never been easy keeping secrets from her. She was absolutely right; I always poured out my heart to her . . . eventually. Came from years of growing up together in Dressel Hills, Colorado. In a tiny ski village like this, it was easier to opt for one best friend over gobs of casual ones. At least for me.

Still, I needed to share my secret with someone. It was so warm and fabulous. Such a beautiful secret should be shared with someone like Andie. I knew she'd be straight with me. I'd never known her to hold back if she felt strongly enough about something. And that's what I needed now, someone who could think clearly about this—whatever it was—that I was feeling for Mr. Barnett.

Danny met me on the stairs as I took two at a time, still hoping to catch Mr. Barnett. His eyes lit up when he saw me. "Are you coming to youth service tonight?" he asked.

I stopped and leaned against the wall, catching my breath. "I think so, why?" Then I remembered his note and my phone call to him. It irritated me. I thought this matter had been settled between us.

Danny hesitated. "We're grouping up for Bible Quiz Team. And . . . I hoped you'd be my partner."

"Me?" I shrieked. "Danny, you've got to be kidding. You can memorize whole chapters of the Bible in one shot. There's no way I can keep up with you."

"I'll help you," he said softly.

That's what I was afraid of. He wanted to tutor me—one on one. Much too cozy. Besides, if I were in the musical, I'd need tons of extra time to memorize my lines. "I'm sorry, Danny. I really can't." I thought of suggesting Paula's twin sister, Kayla, or someone else for him to team up with at church, but I didn't.

Slowly, Danny nodded. "Well, see you around," he said and left.

I was determined not to let his reaction get to me. After all, it was only quiz team.

Thankful the Danny encounter was over, I raced upstairs, hoping to find Mr. Barnett. I thought about casually wandering into the choir room, pretending to sort music or something. Maybe he'd notice and strike up a conversation. But as I approached the door, I knew the mature thing to do was simply knock.

"Come in," he called. His voice sounded much lower than Danny's. Or any other guy's at school, for that matter.

I hesitated, then took a breath for courage and walked in.

"Hi again." He was seated behind the synthesizer, and something about the way he looked up to greet me startled me. Shafts of light from the late afternoon sun streamed through the long, vertical windows behind the choir risers.

I peered round the room. My heart was glowing. Alone with him, in his music room. At last. The hustle-bustle of the school day seemed distant somehow as I returned his smile. With all my heart, I wanted to hold this moment close—memorize it for always.

Still seated behind his keyboard, he motioned to a chair. "Please, sit down." I noticed nut shells strewn on top of his keyboard. "I'm a pistachio nut junkie. Here, have one."

The sheer joy of being here might have left me wordless and clumsy, but like the time of my audition, I felt a strange openness and sense of ease with him. "Thanks," I said, surprised at the way the words spilled out so easily. I took a few nuts and cracked them open.

"So . . . how are things?" he asked. Cool and easy.

"Fine, thanks," I said. *Would it shock him to know I thought of him every waking minute?*

"I'm working on a new song," he remarked. "Tell me what you think." And he began to play. The minor melody drifted down like a mountain brook in June. And when it found a resting place in a gentle broken chord, it took my breath away.

"It's beautiful," I said, longing for more. "It reminds me of a bittersweet book I read once."

"This song is in memory of my grandmother," he said.

I was surprised and pleased that he was sharing such personal information.

"I wish she could hear it." I paused, wondering when I should ask about the interview.

He glanced up at the skylight, neck tilted back slightly. "Sometimes I think she does."

I nodded, smiling. "For me, music paints word pictures. I listen to it when I write."

"My sister's a writer," he said.

"Creativity must run in your family," I said without thinking. "It shows up in the way you teach."

His hands slid off the keyboard and into his lap,

and he leaned back. "You are a very perceptive young woman, Holly."

I felt my cheeks do their usual cherry number, but he looked so pleased with my statement, I didn't let it embarrass me. I pulled out my tablet and pen and asked if he had time for a quick interview. "It's for the school paper. I'm one of the reporters."

"Absolutely," he said. And by the look on his face, I knew Andrew Barnett wasn't just being polite.

5

The interview sailed by, smooth and easy. I asked the usual journalistic questions, prompted by the five Ws. Things like why he'd chosen to major in education, who were his mentors, and what he hoped to do when he graduated from college.

Only once were we interrupted. The janitor came in to empty the trash. Later, I thought I heard the *cre-e-ak* of the door, but when I turned to investigate, no one was there.

Satisfied that the interview was complete, I stood to go. "Thank you for your time, Mr. Barnett. It was nice getting acquainted with you." *If he only knew* . . .

"I've heard you have an excellent way with words, Holly," he said, smiling again. "I'll look forward to seeing your story in *The Lift*."

"Thanks." I reached for my notebook.

He seemed reluctant for me go. "Above all," he

added, "I hope you keep working at your creative goals."

"Thanks," I said again. Slipping my pen into my backpack, I looked up. That's when his eyes met mine. And I knew, sure as anything, something had come alive between us.

♥   ♥   ♥

That night at youth service, a bunch of kids signed up for the Bible Quiz Team. By the looks of the quiz team T-shirts sales, it was a big deal.

"Who're you going to study with?" Stan asked as we came in together. Before I could respond, Andie walked over to him.

"Got a partner yet?" she asked Stan.

He sat down, crossing his long legs. He leaned back and merely grinned.

Here comes John Wayne, I thought. But I was wrong. Today it was Stan Patterson himself. "I'm thinking about it," he said.

Andie giggled, probably holding her breath for him to pick her as his team study partner.

When Danny showed up, I scooted down in my chair. No way could I survive a repeat performance with him. Paula and Kayla Miller arrived just in time, and I waved them over. Paula had established a strong identity all her own. I noticed it as she fluffed her soft shoulder-length curls. Kayla, her twin, seemed content minus the look-alike aspect.

I sighed with relief as I glanced down the row of chairs. Good, no room for Danny to barge in.

Pastor Rob made an announcement. "If you didn't get a Bible Quiz Team card when you came in, please take one home. I'd like each of you to prayerfully consider being on the team or at least help with one of the fund-raisers. We'll be traveling to Denver and Grand Junction for regionals, so it's going to cost us some bucks."

I felt a twinge of guilt as I thought back to the flippant answers I'd given Danny this afternoon. It wasn't the idea of studying and memorizing Scripture that kept me from signing up. It was Danny himself.

Before the youth service ended, I slipped a card into my purse when Danny wasn't watching.

♥   ♥   ♥

The next day was Friday. Audition results! Bypassing my locker, I ran toward the stairs. Had I made it? Was I Maria? Halfway up the stairs, I remembered that I was much too mature to race around the school like this. Slowing to a more sophisticated pace, I made my way toward the music room.

The area was crammed with clusters of kids jockeying for position in front of the music bulletin board. I watched Andie's expression change from curiosity to horror when she saw her name beside the character of Mother Abbess. She'd wanted Maria. Who didn't?

Paula clenched her fists and shook them back and forth with glee when she discovered her name beside Liesl, the oldest daughter of the von Trapp family singers. Liesl, along with Mother Abbess, was a strong supporting role. She'd be playing opposite Stan. Wouldn't Andie die over that matchup?

I could hardly suffer the suspense any longer and pushed through the crowd. Head and shoulders above most of the girls, I could see my name clearly at the top of the list. *Holly Meredith—Maria.* I grinned with delight. This was so perfect.

Just below my name, Jared's name was listed. He was Captain Georg von Trapp. Talk about a nightmare!

Grabbing Andie, I bear-hugged her. "Can you believe it? I'm Maria!" I shouted amid the din of excitement.

She pulled back, glaring. "I should've known."

"Known what?" I demanded, trailing after her.

"C'mon, Holly. Are you brain-dead?" Her tennies slapped against the waxed floor as she hurried toward our lockers.

I grabbed her arm, like *she* usually does to me. "Spell it out, Andie."

She scrunched her face. "Teacher's pet," she snarled. "I saw what you did."

I swallowed hard. Had Andie spied on me doing the interview?

"You thought I was at the Soda Straw with Stan, didn't you?" Her dark eyes flashed with anger. "Well, you were wrong."

"I don't get it," I said, still puzzled.

"I came back to school yesterday to get my math assignment. That's when I ran into Danny, looking pretty lousy. It's none of my business, but what did you say to him?" She took a quick breath. "Never mind. Danny told me you'd gone upstairs. And when I looked for you, there you were in the choir room, shooting the breeze with Mr. Barnett." She wouldn't let me toss a word in edgewise. "How does it feel to bribe a teacher into giving you the lead role?" Her accusing stare made me angry.

"You've got it wrong, Andie," I stated flatly. "You don't know what you're saying."

"Oh yeah?" She slammed her locker. "Guess again."

I couldn't believe it. "Please, don't do this," I said. "You're wrong, it was only an interview."

She didn't hang around to hear more. Off she

flew, down the hall to first period. I opened my locker, refusing to let her childishness spoil my moment.

Maria! I'd actually landed the female lead. I could hardly wait to start working with Mr. Barnett.

♥   ♥   ♥

In science, Mr. Ross droned on about the number of neutrons in a given nucleus. I tried to listen, but this wasn't exactly my favorite subject. It came in a close second to getting my foot stuck in the toilet.

I doodled while the less-than-fascinating lesson continued. *H.M. and A.B.* I wrote calligraphy-style complete with swirls and curls all around . . . and a heart. Mrs. Holly Barnett came next, circled with flowers and vines.

I proceeded to assess the age difference between Mr. Barnett and myself. Fourteen from twenty— only six years. Not bad. In a couple of years, say, when I was eighteen, he'd be twenty-four. That seemed appropriate enough. The older you get, the less the age thing matters. But . . . how could I be sure he'd wait for me to grow up?

Instead of taking notes, I pulled out my tablet from the interview yesterday. I'd have to be careful not to let anything too obvious slip, especially since Andie was on my trail. So far, she'd only accused me of being the teacher's pet. So far . . .

After science, Captain von Jared met me at my locker. "Hello-o, Maria," he sang out, leaning against my locker.

I couldn't help wondering what Mr. Barnett was like when *he* was a junior high student. Surely he had more class than to sing in public, which is what Jared began to do. "How do you solve a problem like Maria?" Right there in the hall with everyone listening. Well, not really listening. Just really staring.

"Knock it off," I said, playfully pushing him aside. "I need to dump some books."

He spied my interview notes. "Hey, what's this?"

I snatched it back. "None of your business."

"Oh, aren't we cute," he teased. "I suppose you expect me to wait till it shows up in *The Lift*."

"It's hardly a rough draft," I shot back.

He leaned over, reading my notes again. "Hey, you're right, this *is* rough. But what can you say about a wimp like Mr. Barnett, anyway?"

I spun around. "A what?"

"You heard me. Barnett's obviously not very good with the ladies, or he'd have latched on to one by now. I mean, what is the guy, twenty-something going on—"

"That's rude," I shot back.

"Okay, so judge me." He ran his fingers through his wavy hair.

"Look, Jared," I huffed, "I've had it with your attitude. Miss Hess thinks we're lucky to have someone like Mr. Barnett doing the drama this year. And so do I." There, now maybe he'd back off.

"Oh, man," Jared whispered, coming closer. He touched my cheek. "I think you're—"

"Get back!" I jerked his hand away.

"I'm sorry, Holly. I didn't mean to—"

"Yes, you did," I retorted.

His voice grew softer. "Look, we'll never pull this musical off if we can't work together."

Jared wasn't kidding. Whether I liked it or not, he and I were stuck with each other. I let go of my sophistication for only a second and groaned audibly, piling my books into my locker.

"C'mon, Holly, give me a break." He grabbed my hand. "It'll be fun, you'll see."

"Right," I muttered, thinking of Mr. Barnett again. Was *he* this immature in eighth grade?

I controlled myself and closed my locker without slamming it. And with as much maturity as I could muster, I walked away from Captain von Disgusting, thinking of a zillion drawbacks to playing opposite him in the spring musical.

I fumed my way into creative writing class. It was going to be horrible—Jared and me together onstage, playing like we were in love. Three weeks ago it wouldn't have been a problem. But now?

Finding my desk, I sat down with a thud. What a nightmare! Jared sat across the aisle to my left, staring at me. I tried to ignore him, but it was hard. Unless I wore blinders, I couldn't help seeing him.

I tried to zero in on Miss Wannamaker's talk. She was discussing humor techniques in writing.

"By bringing two unrelated entities together," she said, "it is possible to surprise the reader. The element of surprise is essential for humor. For instance," and she paused to think. "Ah yes, here's a good example. 'My mother's feet are so big, they have their own zip code.' Feet and zip codes are totally unrelated. So it creates the unexpected, and a good laugh."

She continued giving various examples of surprise twists. I was distracted, however, by Miss W's big, beautiful diamond, her engagement ring from Mr. Ross. It caught the light, nearly blinding me.

Rumor had it their wedding was to be held in the auditorium on the last day of school. A fitting place for two middle-aged teachers to be married, since they'd met here at Dressel Hills Junior High. Visions of white lace, candlelight, and satiny bows flitted in my brain. *Miss W and Mr. Ross.* True love breaks age barriers, no matter where, no matter when.

Jared startled me by holding out a sheet of paper. I shook my head, thinking it was some mushy note of his. But he looked serious, pointing to the words at the top of the page. I felt mighty embarrassed when it turned out to be one of Miss W's handouts. Slipping it into my notebook, I went back to daydreaming about weddings. This time it was mine. And Andrew Barnett's. Someday . . .

I didn't dare close my eyes in class, but staring at the clouds would do. Zipping through time and space, I was now twenty-two, the perfect age for a girl like me to say "I do." It was, after all, the age of my mother when she married my father. Andrew, at twenty-eight, had eagerly, but patiently, waited for me to graduate from high school and finish college. Now, the proud owner of a degree in English, I planned to write scripts for Andrew's musicals once he and I had united our hearts in wedded bliss.

I stood by his side in front of an altar flanked with white roses. All shimmery in white organza and lace, I gazed into my groom's eyes. On cue, he went to the keyboard and played his lovely song, written especially for our wedding. Strains of the haunting love song filled the sunny mountain chapel.

Soon the minister posed the important question. "Do you, Andrew Barnett, take Holly Meredith to be your wedded wife?"

"I do," Andrew answered. He smiled sweetly.

The minister turned to me and asked, "Do you, Holly Meredith, take Jared Wilkins—"

Jared Wilkins?

Inwardly, I shrieked as Jared's boyish face appeared before me, in front of the flower-draped altar.

"Jared Wilkins," Miss W was calling his name.

Snapping to attention, I jerked back to reality as Jared stood at the front of the class, preparing to read. By the looks of things, we'd had an assignment while I was planning my future.

I listened carefully as Jared read, trying to decipher the assignment. The class laughed as he read his clever combinations of unrelated entities. Maybe, just maybe, if I hurried, I could catch up with the class before someone called on me.

I searched through my notebook for the handout Jared had given me earlier. By the time I found it and read the assignment, it was too late to put anything on paper.

Miss W called my name. "Holly, will you please read your work to the class?" Startled and completely unprepared, I looked up at her. She adjusted her glasses, studying me. She knew.

"I'm sorry, Miss Wannamaker," I confessed. "I'm not ready."

She cast her angelic smile my way. "Holly, this isn't like you." She walked toward my desk. "Do you understand the assignment?"

I understood, all right. I'd been caught daydreaming, and she was making a point of it. Being the wonderful teacher she was, Miss W didn't embarrass me, but she did pat my arm in a concerned sort of way as she called on Marcia Green, the smartest student in school.

Jared slid into his seat, motioning to me with his hands, palms turned up. "What's going on?" he whispered.

I turned away, ignoring him as I stared at the blank sheet of paper in front of me. My daydreaming had just put a black mark on my record. I hoped Miss W wouldn't count it against me when it came time for the semester grade.

When the bell rang, Jared waited for me by the door. "I heard we're having the first read-through on act one today after school."

"We are?"

"Mr. Barnett said to pass the word." Jared held the door for me as we headed for the hall. Reluctantly, I walked with him through the halls toward history class. On the way, I saw my mom with Stephie, my stepsister, heading upstairs.

"What are you doing here?" I asked, surprised.

"Miss Hess is having tryouts for the younger von Trapp children this morning," Mom said. "Stephie's dying for a chance at it, so I took her out of school."

Stephie nodded. "I'm going to be Marta." Mischief danced from her eyes.

I blurted my exciting news. "And *I'm* going to be Maria."

Mom threw her arms around me in front of Jared and everyone. "That's absolutely wonderful, Holly-Heart."

Jared grinned, waiting for me to tell *his* news, no doubt.

Stephie came to my rescue. "Aren't you supposed to tell me to break my foot or something?"

Jared nodded. "Close enough."

Mom remembered Jared. "Hello, again," she said to him. "Are you in the musical?"

Was he ever!

"Yes, ma'am," he replied. "I'll be playing the part of Captain von Trapp."

Mom's eyes twinkled as she put two and two together. "Oh, Holly," she said. "So this is your leading man."

I glanced at my watch. "Well, I better get to class." I was eager to end this cozy conversation before Mom had me linked up with Jared all over again. "See you after school. Good luck on your audition, Stephie."

"Bye, Holly," Stephie called after me.

Jared seemed more than anxious to keep up with me. "Mind if I walk the leading lady to class?"

I tossed my hair. "I'll walk myself, thanks." My pledge to abandon the boys my age was still in force. Besides, what if Mr. Barnett met up with us? It was too risky.

Jared was right; Mr. Barnett began spreading the word to everyone involved in act one of the play. If possible, we were to meet in the choir room after school. I told Andie about it when I saw her at lunch. "It's going to be so-o fabulous," I said.

Still fuming, she pretended not to pay attention.

"Okay," I said. "Have it your way. But I thought nuns took the vow of celibacy, not silence." That got her going.

"Holly Meredith, you think you're so smart because you got Maria's part," she retorted, looking to Stan for moral support. But he only made matters worse by waving Paula over to their table.

Andie made a face, but Stan laughed it off. "After all, if Paula's going to be my girlfriend in the musical, don't you think I oughta get acquainted with her?"

Leave it to Stan to get himself into hazardous situations. Andie began twisting a curl around her finger. Man, was he in trouble now!

"Just relax, Andie," I heard Stan say as I turned to go. "It's only a play."

Only a play? I thought. It was much more than that. It was the path that led to Mr. Barnett. And nothing—not Andie, and certainly not Jared— could keep me from walking it.

7

A bunch of kids showed up for the read-through of act one. Students took turns sitting around a long table. I sat at the opposite end, away from Jared. Characters who appeared in later scenes sat on the risers, observing.

When it came time for the third scene, where Andie portrays the Mother Abbess, we cracked up. She really hammed it up, especially when she came to the part about Maria being a good choice for a governess. "Look here, Sister Maria twit," she ad-libbed. "I'm sick and tired of the way you're causing problems around here, trying to catch clouds, flibb-ity-jibbiting your way through morning prayers . . ." Andie crossed her eyes and looked down her nose at me, raising her voice to a ridiculously high pitch. "Are you catching my drift?"

"Andie," Mr. Barnett cut in. "Please read your lines more carefully."

I snickered, watching his face, serious and drawn, loving every second of this sudden revelation of strength. It was as though Mr. Barnett was allowing his character to be revealed, layer by wondrous layer.

When it was time for my lines, Mr. Barnett stopped me numerous times. Not because he had a problem with what I was doing, but because he wanted to interact with me. Why else?

On one occasion, he even acted out Jared's part of the scene with me. I watched his face light up as we exchanged dialogue. It was so obvious. Genuine interest was written all over his face. Was this the beginning of my dream come true?

♥　♥　♥

Mr. Barnett gave final instructions before we left. "I want lines for this act memorized in two weeks." I wondered how I'd juggle homework and a zillion lines between now and then.

I headed for the bus stop with Andie, Paula, and Kayla. That's when Andie jumped all over me. "It's really too bad you and Jared broke up, you know. This could've been so-o romantic," she crooned.

Paula wasn't quite as direct, but she had an opinion, all right. "I have a great idea. Why couldn't you and Jared act a little friendlier offstage, at least for the sake of the play?"

Some nerve!

"Look, you two," I said, irritated beyond my limits of mature behavior, "if you think Jared's so fabulous and wonderful ... well, have at it." Boiling with anger, I pulled on my hair clasp, and my hair came pouring down. "He's all yours."

I halfway expected Paula to take me up on it. Not too long ago she'd been crazy over Jared. Now that he was free for the taking, she didn't even seem interested.

I sat in the back of the bus by myself, while Andie and Paula crowded in with Kayla. Periodically, they turned and scowled their disapproval.

Fine, I thought, staring at the back of their heads. *Go ahead, behave like the children you are.*

♥   ♥   ♥

At home, Stephie met me at the front door, squealing her excitement. "I'm going to be in *The Sound of Music!*"

"That's perfect," I said, swinging her around. "We can practice the 'Do-Re-Mi' song together."

She nodded, taking my hand and pulling me

into the kitchen. Mom looked up from her desk in the corner.

"Mommy made snickerdoodles for us to celebrate," Stephie announced.

"I think she's become an addict," Mom said, laughing. "Like you."

I picked out three extra-round cookies before settling down at the bar. "Mmm, perfect."

"Thought you'd be ready for something sweet," Mom said, handing me an envelope. "This came in the mail today."

I recognized the handwriting. "It's from Daddy."

I hurried to the knife rack and sliced the envelope open.

"Careful Maria doesn't cut herself," Stephie teased.

"Yes, Marta," I answered.

Stephie seemed pleased with herself as she snatched up a handful of cookies and disappeared downstairs.

Letters from California were coming more frequently these days. Especially since Daddy's visit to Dressel Hills a few weeks ago. Carrie and I had spent the entire day skiing with him, making happy memories. About time. Almost six years had passed since he and Mom split up. We had some major catching up to do.

I pulled the letter out slowly, curious about Daddy's life in California, as always.

Dear Holly,

Thanks for your letter. I always enjoy hearing from you. Carrie too. Please share this letter with her.

My reason for writing is to tell you some wonderful news. When you were here last Christmas, we talked about my investigation into the New Testament. Well, after many weeks of reading the Gospels (several times, I must say), I've been pondering the teachings found in them.

Last week, I accepted Christ as my Savior during a Christian businessmen's luncheon. I wanted you to be one of the first to know.

I stopped reading and looked over at Mom, who was sorting coupons at the kitchen desk. "Daddy's become a Christian," I said solemnly.

Mom leaped off the chair, coupons scattering everywhere. She peered over my shoulder.

"See?" I pointed to his words.

"That's wonderful," she said. Her smile warmed my heart.

I finished reading Daddy's letter.

Many times I recalled your words, Holly, the ones you said that night in the Los Angeles chapel, nearly a year ago. Do you remember?

I stopped reading, thinking back. He and Saundra, his new wife, had come to hear me sing while I was on tour with the church youth choir in California. After the concert, Daddy and I talked quietly on the second pew of the sanctuary while the risers and sound equipment were being carried out to the bus. He'd held my hand as we discussed his sister, my aunt Marla, and her death. For a precious moment I had felt close to my estranged father.

I continued reading:

> *I'll never forget what you said, Holly: "I've been praying for you all this time," you told me. How grateful I am that you never gave up on your terrible old man.*

What did he mean, terrible? He had no way of knowing what I knew about his and Mom's divorce. In fact, it had only been a few weeks since Mom and I had the mother of all heart-to-heart talks. Shocking as the truth was, it boiled down to two major problems. Daddy had been determined to move to California. Wanted to uproot the family to pursue his career in another state without taking Mom's aversion to big cities into consideration. She was stubborn, too, and wouldn't agree to go. Ultimately, she sent him on ahead, by himself, secretly hoping he'd get his fill of the mad-dash executive lifestyle in a few months. But Mom's plan backfired. Daddy had thrived on the fast pace and never returned.

At that time, neither of them were Christians. Mom found it difficult to give in to Daddy's desire to move. But that wasn't the only problem. My father was proud and sorely hurt. When Mom had a miscarriage and asked him to come back to Dressel Hills while she was hospitalized, Daddy refused. Evidently he wasn't interested in having more children anyway, and his selfish reaction to her request was the straw that broke the marriage.

Stubborn and angry, they agreed to divorce, leaving Carrie and me without a father. And with a hollow ache in our hearts.

Of course, I didn't know all this at age eight, but now I was much more mature. Was I mature enough to forgive Daddy for leaving? I sighed, thinking back to the many years of nightly prayers. For Daddy . . .

For all of us.

I folded the letter and carefully slipped it back into the envelope. Daddy was a Christian now—the answer to my dearest prayer. So, why wasn't I dancing for joy?

I joined Mom at the sink. She whittled away at a long, fat carrot, flicking curly shavings into a bowl.

"The Lord answered my prayer," I said softly.

Mom nodded, and letting the peeler fall into the sink with a clatter, she reached out to me. For a long, sweet moment we held each other. Mom stroked my hair, whispering "Holly-Heart" over and over. Her soothing voice and her gentle perfume erased my worry. If only for a moment.

In a strange sort of way, the timing of his conversion upset me. It had taken all these years to find out the truth, and just when I was ready to unload on him, ready to fire questions at him about the rotten way he'd abandoned us, he decided to become a follower of Jesus Christ.

God had forgiven Daddy. Wasn't I supposed to do the same?

8

Supper was plain boring. Not because the Spanish rice and fixings weren't delicious. It had to do with living in limbo, waiting for the weekend to melt into Monday, when I would see Mr. Barnett again.

Grabbing my journal, I let Carrie do kitchen cleanup while I headed for the porch swing to record my thoughts. The last rays of the sun warmed my back as I drifted back and forth, thinking through the amazing events of the past week. My attraction to Mr. Barnett was more than a silly crush. Much more.

If I had to get a crush on someone, it easily could have been Pastor Rob, or the boys' basketball coach. But Mr. Barnett . . . Hmm. What was it about him, anyway?

I opened my journal. *Friday, April 15. If my friends knew my secret, they'd die laughing. Especially*

Jared. Danny too. I'm sure Danny would think my feelings for Andrew Barnett are totally illogical. But so what? I don't care!

I looked up, staring at the clouds. Logical or not, my feelings were strong. They'd been growing since last Monday when Andrew Barnett's world collided with mine—when he looked into my eyes and saw the real me. Holly Meredith . . . the emerging, mature me.

He surely liked what he'd seen. I could tell by the way he looked at me, the way he spoke to me. After all, if an intelligent college man had singled me out from the rest of the girls at school, it was proof. Proof that something was happening in me. Proof that I was more grown-up than the others.

I lay down on the swing, letting its gentle swaying lull me into a daydreamy place where it was safe to concoct elaborate scenes. Warm, cozy scenes featuring Andrew and me. He looked into my eyes, sharing the secrets of his life, his dreams, his goals. Yet he seemed to see how wonderful I was, too.

Then we walked together, in a wooded area near a pond, talking about nature and life and God. He listened, admiring my adult view of life, and my faith. Beneath the moonlit sky, he held my hand, clasping it warmly in his.

Andie's loud whistle caught me off guard. The daydream tumbled down as she plopped onto the chaise lounge across from me. "Whatcha doin'?" she asked, smoothing her canary yellow Capri pants.

I sat up on the swing, stretching, surprised to see her. "Nothin' much." I held my journal close.

She glanced at me, wistful eyes acknowledging her curiosity. "Anything going on?" She pulled her knees up under her chin.

"Nope," I said, wondering if now was a good time to test my secret on her. "Just catching up on my journal, that's all."

"Oh," she said, her voice trailing off. "Thought I'd come over. Nothing's happening at home. I tried to call . . . your phone's tied up."

"Stan's hogging it," I commented without thinking. Now she'd probably launch off on her jealous routine.

"Who with?" I was right, she *had* to know. "Better not be Paula. She gives me the creeps being Liesl in the play. You know she has that long, lovey-dovey scene with Stan."

This was so childish. Why wasn't I surprised?

"What do you think of Mr. Barnett?" I heard myself saying.

"Him?" Andie shrugged. "He's okay, I guess. Might make a good teacher someday."

"Might?" I snapped.

"He's so . . . so serious. Kinda like you've been lately." She was using one of her best tactics to get me talking.

"What's wrong with that?" I crossed my legs and pulled them under me.

"It's not like you, Holly."

"You're wrong. I *am* serious," I said. "Much more than you know."

Andie cocked her head, studying me. "This is about something else. Mr. Barnett, right?"

Hearing his name took my breath away. "I think he's a wonderful teacher," I said softly.

Andie raised her hands to the sky. "Not another crush, and on an older guy, no less. Didn't you learn anything from your fiasco with that pen pal, Lucas Leigh?"

"This is different," I answered.

Andie put her hands behind her head. "Well, I've got all night." She leaned back. "So what's going on with you and Barnett?"

"He likes me," I said defensively.

"I know—you're the teacher's pet!" She wasn't taking me seriously.

I turned my head and looked at the front yard, gray in the fading light of dusk. Cunningly, I steered the conversation away from Mr. Barnett by telling her about Daddy's conversion.

"That's so great, Holly. It's what you've been living for all these years," she said. "What about his wife?"

"He didn't mention her in the letter, so I don't know."

Andie leaned forward, her eyes boring a hole in me.

"You're not so thrilled about this. How come?"

"Are you kidding?" I said, hoping Andie would drop it, now that she knew. After the way she acted about Mr. Barnett, I wasn't eager to tell her anything else personal.

Mom stepped out on the porch with a glass candle holder and matches. "It's getting dark," she said. "Thought this might be more fun than a porch light."

"Thanks, Mom." I watched her light the candle and set it on the white wicker table beside the chaise.

"Is anyone using the phone now?" Andie asked her.

Mom glanced through the screen door. "I believe it's free, but you'd better grab it quick."

Andie excused herself and went inside. When she came back, Stan was with her. "We're going for ice cream, wanna come?" she asked.

"Not tonight," I said, getting up. "I have tons of lines to memorize."

"Did you sign up for the car wash next weekend?" she asked as they hurried down the steps. "We could use some more help."

"Sure, I'll help," I said.

"See you at church Sunday," Andie called to me before getting into the family van.

"Okay, see ya," I said, hugging my diary tightly.

♥ ♥ ♥

On Saturday, I took a break from learning lines and rode my bike downtown. Paula and Kayla were out jogging around the courthouse grounds.

"Holly, hey!" called Paula when she saw me. Her hair was pulled back in a tight little bun. Kayla waved as she matched her pace with Paula's. Their long legs moved in identical motion, glazed with sweat.

I pedaled hard to catch up with them, then coasted, free and easy, careful not to crowd them or throw off their rhythm.

"Looks like you guys are serious about this," I said as we made another lap around the courthouse.

"It's Miss Tucker's idea," Kayla said. "She's desperate for runners this season."

We circled the grounds again. Aspen leaves rippled, robins sang in chorus, and the Miller twins panted, out of breath.

At last we slowed our pace, coming to a stop. I dropped the kickstand down on my bike and sat on the courthouse lawn. Paula jogged in place, puffing spurts of air, slowly lowering her pulse rate. Kayla swung her arms wide around her, back and forth, running in place, creating a human windmill.

I pulled *The Sound of Music* script out of my backpack. "Sometimes I wonder why I ever wanted to be Maria," I complained, watching the twins do their stretches. "I didn't realize how much work it would be."

"You should join the track team if you think sitting around memorizing lines is tough," Kayla said.

"Track's not for me," I confessed. "But I can't wait to read through act two on Monday." I pulled on a blade of grass.

"Anxious to see Mr. Barnett?" Paula teased.

I bit on the end of my hair. "What do you mean?"

"That you have a thing for him," she said, flashing her perfect pearly whites.

Kayla perked up. "Is it true?"

"Where'd you hear such a thing?" I asked.

Paula's eyes widened. "I can't imagine Andie making up something like this."

A cold shiver swept over me. "Andie told you that?" *Some friend!*

Embarrassed at our conversation, Kayla looked away, digging into her shorts for a ponytail band.

I stood up, brushing the grass off my shorts. "Look, I don't know what kind of info Andie's feeding you, but what I told her was I think Mr. Barnett's a wonderful teacher. That's it."

"Okay, okay," Paula said. "It's no big deal then, is it?"

No big deal when you've just discovered your best friend can't be trusted? How could Andie do this to me?

9

I ignored Andie as much as possible the next few days. Every single minute I had my head buried in my script. Besides that, after-school rehearsals and the article featuring Mr. Barnett kept me super busy. Because of a slight lull in homework assignments, I managed to turn *The Lift* story in well before the deadline.

My attraction to Mr. Barnett had grown to monumental proportions in just a short time. Not only had I included his name on my prayer list, he was showing up in my dreams, too.

Car wash day, Saturday, April 23, dawned sunny and hot, so I wore my jean shorts. By helping to raise money, I was doing my part for Danny and the quiz team. No way could I be Danny's partner and still be true to my feelings for Mr. Barnett.

Danny showed up first thing, before any of the others. "Need some help?" he asked as I searched in

Pastor Rob's pickup for an extension cord.

"I'm sure it's around here somewhere," I said, hoping I wouldn't be stuck with Danny all day. Not surprisingly, he didn't take the hint, and scurried around searching for it anyway. Finally he located the longest cord the church owned.

"Good, we're in business," he said.

Then Jared showed up. Now it was the three of us. Working as a team, we washed cars and vacuumed their interiors. By midmorning I was wiped out. "Can you cover for me?" I asked the guys.

"Glad to," Danny said, wiping the perspiration from his forehead.

"Take your time," Jared called to me.

I chuckled at their childish attempts to impress me—something I couldn't imagine Andrew Barnett doing in a zillion years. Digging into my shorts for some cash, I headed to the nearest pop machine. I poked the appropriate selection and waited for the machine to do its thing. Nothing happened. Gently, I tapped on the selection button again.

"Kick it."

I turned to see Andie. "Where'd you come from?"

"My dad just dropped me off," she said. "Still mad at me?"

" 'Course not." I pushed the coin return. Coins clattered down and I picked them up to try again. "But I still can't believe you told Paula about our private conversation." I glanced around, hoping no one was listening. "It was supposed to be confidential."

"What, that you think you-know-who's wonderful? I thought you meant it was like some little crush. I mean, it's nothing like the real thing, is it?"

My face felt hot. "Well, no. I'm not in love, if that's what you mean." I felt wicked, betraying him that way. "It was a private matter, Andie, and I expected you to act grown-up enough to keep it to yourself. I mean, hey, if I can't trust you, who can I trust?"

Andie grabbed my arm. "Look, I'm sorry. Paula's the only one I told, honest."

Could I believe that?

"It's the truth, you can ask anyone here," she said with a straight face.

"Why, you!"

Just then my pop can came rumbling down.

"Saved by a Pepsi," she said, laughing.

I couldn't help myself, I laughed with her. It dispelled my anger, the anger I'd bottled up inside me all week.

As I drank the soda, two more customers drove in. "Guess we'd better get busy," I said, spotting a baby-blue Thunderbird.

"Wow, would you look at that," Andie said, staring at the 1957 classic Thunderbird sports car. We stood there watching as Danny and Jared ran over to inspect the beautiful old car.

"Perfect, maybe now I can work in peace, without Danny breathing down my neck," I muttered. I tilted my head back and took a long, slow drink of the ice-cold soda.

"Only if you're lucky," Andie snickered and ran over to check out the T-Bird.

Still sipping my soda, I straddled the log bench. That's when the door on the car opened. Out stepped Mr. Barnett!

I swallowed my pop too fast and the fizz went up my nose. Coughing, I ran inside the gas station to the ladies' room. I yanked on the toilet paper and blew my nose. Before I left, I checked my hair and makeup. It was no use; I'd left my purse at home. Embarrassed and nervous, I headed back outside.

"Holly," called Danny, motioning to me. "Can you vac this one out?"

"Sure," I said, hurrying over to the T-Bird.

Mr. Barnett was under the hood, showing Jared and Billy the engine. Danny, conscientious as always, began soaping up the car with his giant sponge.

I pressed the button on the vacuum canister and began to clean the inside of Mr. Barnett's glorious old car. The two-seater had been refurbished, by the looks of things. Nothing *this* ancient could still be in such good shape. Pieces of lint and pebbles of dirt had found their way onto the floor of the driver's side. Other than that, the interior was immaculate.

I balanced my pop can in one hand and gave the passenger's side a going-over even though it looked spotless. It was obvious no one had sat there recently. *Must mean he doesn't have a girlfriend,* I reasoned.

I could hear Mr. Barnett talking about the V-8 engine and how it could get up and go on the road. It struck me as special—taking time to introduce the guys to the mechanics of a fifties sports car.

Peeking through the crack in the hood, I could see Mr. Barnett's face. Gentle, sweet. I leaned against the dash, sighing. Not wanting him to see me, I pretended to put my pop on the dash as an excuse for being so close to the windshield.

That's when it happened. I accidentally pressed the button for the glove compartment, and it flew open.

"Oh no," I whispered, fumbling to pick up its contents, hoping Mr. Barnett wouldn't choose this moment to close the hood. As long as it was up, with him under it, showing off the engine, I was safe.

Hurriedly, I stuffed a note pad and pen, several maps of Colorado, and an address book back into the roomy compartment. I checked under the seat to make sure I'd found everything. Two snapshots had strayed from sight, and I reached to rescue them. Pulling them out of hiding, I stole a quick look.

Mr. Barnett and a beautiful woman posed on an arched bridge over a small stream. Willow trees draped their branches around the smiling couple. I swallowed hard as I shuffled the second photo on top. The people looked the same, but this time Mr. Barnett had his arms around the slender woman, hugging her playfully.

Ka-whack! The hood came down. Startled, I jumped, dropping the pictures. Mr. Barnett was coming around the driver's side. He'd catch me snooping for sure.

Without thinking, I slammed the glove compartment and bent the pictures just enough to let the vacuum hose suck up the evidence.

"Holly!" Mr. Barnett called over the noise of the vacuum. "I had no idea you were in here." He leaned on the window, smiling warmly.

Forcing a smile, I punched the Off button on the vacuum, thinking only of the swallowed-up pictures, deep inside the cavernous cleaner. "I like your car," my boring words came out. It's hard to be eloquent when you're frantic with worry, not to mention having to deal with the pain of coming face-to-face with another woman. Snapshot or not.

"Who's collecting the bucks for the wash job?" Mr. Barnett asked, admiring the job Danny had done.

"You can give the money to me," Danny said. "I'll see that it gets into the Bible quiz fund."

Mr. Barnett came around to my side of the car, where I was securing the vacuum cleaner attachments, preparing for the next job. He reached into his pants pocket and pulled a ten-dollar bill from his billfold. I couldn't help noticing the face of the woman in the front of his billfold, safely snuggled in the little wallet window. The *same* woman.

I drew a faltering breath as I looked away, enduring the heart pain. Why hadn't I suspected something like this before?

Andie came over just then. "You look tired," she said. "Why don't you take a break?"

"I need to check the vacuum cleaner." I rolled it away from Mr. Barnett's car. Andie followed me as Danny and Mr. Barnett stood talking. I whispered to Andie through clenched teeth, "Stand in front of me and don't make a big deal about this."

Her eyebrows gathered into a frown. "What's going on?"

I wanted to cry. "Just don't say anything," I warned her, reaching inside the canister's cone and pulling out the snapshots. "Whew, that was close." I wiped the dust off the pictures with my shirttail. "They're only slightly bent."

I heard Mr. Barnett start his car and let the engine idle. Without rehearsing my words, I dashed over to the passenger's side of the car, waving the pictures.

He leaned over and wound down the window, looking puzzled.

"These got vacuumed up, accidentally." It was the truth. Sort of.

"That's weird, but thanks." A slight frown appeared.

"I'm really sorry, Mr. Barnett. I'll be happy to pay you for reprints, or whatever," I offered.

He took the pictures from me. "Don't worry about it, Holly." He looked up at me, smiling, breaking my heart.

"I'm sorry," I said again, wiping my forehead on my sleeve.

Andie called to me, "Who was supposed to pick up hamburgers for everyone?"

"Oh, *that's* what I forgot," I said. "I'll run down to McDonald's and be back in no time."

"Why do that?" Mr. Barnett said. "I'd be glad to drive you." He leaned over and opened the car door. "What about you, Andie?" He looked at her. "Ever ride in an old jalopy?"

Andie shook her head. "We're a little short-handed here. But thanks." She waved, grinning from ear to ear. I knew what was going through her mind. She'd declined so I could be the one to ride with Mr. Barnett. And I loved her for it.

One of my daydreams had come true. Maybe Mr.

Barnett would whisk me away, dump the other girl, of course, and we'd live happily ever. . . .

I hesitated, leaning on the car door.

"The jalopy's safe, Holly," he teased. "I rebuilt the engine myself." He opened the glove compartment and pushed the pictures out of sight.

My heart skipped a beat. And without another thought, I stepped into Mr. Barnett's Thunderbird.

10

The breeze from the windows blew my hair as we rode toward Aspen Street. The Golden Arches was only a mile or so away. I tried to imagine going on a date with Mr. Barnett, maybe with the convertible top down, the wind blowing our hair, his arm resting on the back of my seat.

He glanced at me as we stopped for a red light. "What do you think of my great-aunt's Thunderbird?"

"Well, I've never really seen one this close before," I said. "But I think your aunt has good taste in old cars."

"Better than that," he said with a smile. "She left it to me in her will. I doubt she knew the value of it, though."

"Looks like she took good care of it."

"Aunt Edna was like that. She hung on to all kinds of things. My sister does the same thing." He chuckled softly. "Those pictures you rescued," and he pointed to the glove box, "are of my sis and me outside Aunt Edna's place, before my aunt died last year."

"Your sister?" My heart sang. "She's beautiful," I said, certain I would never have admitted that if she'd turned out to be his girlfriend.

"Janna's five years older than I am. She's finishing up a double master's program this quarter," he said proudly.

"I'm impressed." I pushed a strand of hair back behind my ear, wondering how I was doing holding up my end of the conversation.

He leaned his arm out the window. "She's a very special girl." He paused. "You remind me of her when she was your age."

Things were so comfortable between us, like we'd known each other all our lives.

"How's it feel having an older sister?" I asked.

"Oh, things aren't much different than if she and I were close in age. At least not now. I guess that's the way it is ... as people grow up, the age barriers drop away." He signaled to turn, smiling broadly, almost winking. But then again, maybe the sun was in his eyes. "I see that Danny fellow is hanging around," he continued.

I knew what he was getting at. "Yeah, Danny and I went out last summer," I said.

"Looks to me like he's still interested."

Was Mr. Barnett jealous?

I sighed. "Actually, Danny and I are just good friends now." I had to let Mr. Barnett know, in no uncertain terms, the status between Danny and me. I relaxed a bit as we pulled into McDonald's.

"Danny's older, right?"

"Only a year," I said, wishing we'd get off this subject.

"Well, I have a question for you, Holly. What do you think when one person is older than the other . . . if he likes the other person but isn't totally certain the feelings are mutual?" He paused, turning off the ignition, looking at me.

It thrilled me to know he was thinking of us, our age difference, that is. If he was cool with the age thing, well . . . so was I.

"I've read about romance when one person's lots older." I hesitated, trying to remember the book I'd read. "I think it helps if one of them gives the other a sign."

He looked blank, confused.

I tried to explain. "You know, a sort of message . . . from one heart to another." It sounded corny, but it sure worked in the book. Besides, it gave me a fabulous idea. The perfect idea!

We walked into McDonald's together, and when he held the door for me, my sleeve touched his sleeve, sending electricity down my arm. I could scarcely manage to answer him when he asked how

many hamburgers to order. But I got it together soon
enough and stepped up to the counter.

♥   ♥   ♥

On the way back to the car wash, I clasped the
large sacks of warm cheeseburgers and fries. My
mind felt numb, paralyzed by our precious moments
together. Mr. Barnett had said so much in only a few
sentences. Now it was my turn to respond, to say or
do something that would let him know that he was
special to me, too. But what?

He turned on the radio to the only oldies station
in Dressel Hills. His smile made my heart leap. "So
what do you think, riding in a hot old T-Bird?"

I shook my head, not quite able to look at him,
but the warm, easy way about him unlocked my
brain and I heard myself say, "Thanks for driving me
to McDonald's." It wasn't what I really wanted to
say. Not even close.

"My pleasure." He turned onto the street where
the car wash kids were probably dying of starvation.
Precious seconds were slipping away as Aunt Edna's
classic Thunderbird sports car purred down the tree-
lined street.

"When do we start blocking the musical
onstage?" I blurted, longing to fill each remaining

moment with the sound of his voice.

He nodded. "Very soon. And we've got such a fantastic cast," he said, flashing his grin at me. "You're perfect for Maria, you know."

I blushed. "Thanks. I really like this musical." I liked something, *someone* else, too, but when I started to say it straight out, I changed my mind. There was a much better way.

We drove into the car wash area, and Danny and Jared came running up like raving maniacs before Mr. Barnett could stop the car. So typical of boys their age. By the way they were salivating, you'd think they hadn't eaten in days. They grabbed several sacks overflowing with cheeseburgers and fries and headed for the shade of the gas station. Andie, Paula, and Kayla came dashing over as I got out of the car. Amy-Liz, Joy, and Shauna were close behind.

"Thanks again, Mr. Barnett," I called, keeping things businesslike, hoping no one suspected anything.

"I hope your church makes a lot of money for the quiz team."

"Good-bye," I said.

"I'll see you Monday," he called, honking his car out on the street. All of us waved as he sped away.

"*I'll see you Monday*" still echoed in my brain as I handed three sacks of food to the girls. "There should be plenty for everyone," I said.

"What, no ketchup?" Andie asked, digging into the sack.

"It's in there somewhere," I said, following her over to the grassy area behind the gas station.

We girls sat together, gobbling down our lunch. Several parents from the church took over the car wash operation while we ate. And Danny, eating with the guys, kept glancing over every so often. *Now* what was he thinking?

After we finished eating, I dragged Andie into the ladies' rest room. "We *have* to talk," I whispered.

"I'm dying for details. And don't tell me your brain froze up and you forgot them."

"There's no way I'll ever forget," I said, locking the bathroom door behind us. "I've stored his words away forever." I patted my heart.

"Spare the dramatics," she said. "Get to the facts."

I told her everything, even what Mr. Barnett had said about our age difference not being a problem.

"You've got to be kidding!"

"Cross my heart, and hope—"

"Don't say that, Holly. Grow up," she said.

"I have." And I knew it was true just as sure as I knew Mr. Barnett and I would be together forever. Someday.

11

It didn't take long to think through my plan once I arrived home. In the safety of my bedroom, a deliciously warm feeling settled over me as I wrote in my journal. *Saturday, April 23: This is the best day of my life! Something fabulous happened today. I rode in Andrew Barnett's beautiful baby-blue Thunderbird. It was like we were supposed to spend the time together, talking about our age difference in private. The way Andrew sees it, his being older is not a problem. But now, I must let him know I agree with him. And I have the most fabulous idea. More later . . .*

I tucked my diary safely away in my bottom dresser drawer. That's when I heard Mom's little dinner bell.

"Supper will be ready in fifteen minutes," she called.

I grabbed some clean clothes and raced to the bathroom, hurrying to clean up. While in the shower, I decided I would compose my written response to Andrew Barnett after supper. It should be anonymous. Besides, he'd surely know it was from me.

♥   ♥   ♥

After supper, Carrie and I brought the leftovers from the dining room into the kitchen. "Have you written back to Daddy yet?" she asked.

"I've been too busy," I said, not eager to talk about it. "Haven't had time with all the rehearsals for the musical."

"Mommy told me that Grandma Meredith says he's going to church every Sunday."

"That's good." And it really was, but I still couldn't deal with my hidden anger toward him. He'd hurt my mother big time, and now that I knew exactly what had happened to cause the divorce, I couldn't just overlook his sins and forgive him. Only God could do that.

"Saundra goes along to church with him sometimes," she continued. "Tyler too."

"Really? That's great." I'd been hoping my stepmother might open up to spiritual things. And I wasn't surprised about Tyler. He'd been full of questions about God and creation and the Bible ever since day one—since last summer, when I first went to California to visit Daddy.

Carrie headed back into the dining room, nearly bumping into Mom, who looked slightly peeved at Uncle Jack. He was piled high with plates. Dirty napkins were scrunched under one hand. He tossed a strained grin at Mom. "Here comes the other partner in the Share the Housework Team," he said.

"After four and a half months of marriage, it's about time," she said sarcastically.

With great fanfare, he balanced the dirty dishes, placing them carefully on the counter. Hurrying over to the freezer, he pulled out the ice-cube trays. "Aha, just as I thought. Empty again!" And with boyish delight, he rushed to the sink and filled the trays with water, as though he were doing something very important for the family.

Mom looked like she wanted to continue scowling, but when Uncle Jack closed the freezer, with the newly filled ice-cube trays safely tucked away, he tiptoed over to Mom and gave her a hug. She giggled as he planted a kiss on her neck, and I knew their tiff over household chores was past.

I didn't see what the big fuss was anyway. After all, I'd seen Uncle Jack helping around the kitchen occasionally, fixing meals. If you can classify meals as something involving important ingredients like peanut butter and jelly. I'd seen him help in the kitchen at least three or four times since they'd married. So what was the big deal?

Maybe the honeymoon stage was starting to dissipate. Maybe now they would start acting normal. Like other married people.

I heard Mom say, "Can we talk?" while smothered in Uncle Jack's arms.

It was my cue to disappear, dishes or not. Thrilled at the chance to exit, I ran to my room.

Closing the door, I wished for a lock, but the lack of one didn't keep me from pulling out my prettiest stationery and settling in at my desk. Important stuff like this must be thought out carefully, so I wrote the first draft on scratch paper.

At last, I was ready to transfer my words to my flowery paper, which just happened to have hearts scattered all around.

Dear Andrew, I began. It was important to address him by his first name since he'd gone out of his way to let me know how special he thought I was. After all, weren't we already sort of together in our hearts?

What a fabulous job you're doing on The Sound of Music. *Thanks for working so hard to make it a success.*

I couldn't work my way into the nitty-gritty without some sort of compliment.

Also, thanks for sharing your thoughts with me Saturday. It meant a lot.

I have a great idea. Let's get together sometime and discuss things further. Maybe over coffee or tea?

I chose coffee because that's what adults usually say when they want an excuse to tie up a restaurant booth for at least an hour. And tea? That's what Mom drinks when her nerves are frayed. The peppermint variety. Andrew might understand the tea thing, especially if he was at all nervous about another encounter with me.

In keeping with my original plan, I decided not to sign my name, but wrote: *Most sincerely, You-know-who*.

Ecstatic about my plan, I folded the stationery and slid it into a matching envelope. I didn't lick it. Not yet. It was only Saturday night and Monday seemed far away. Who knows? I might want to read the note again—so I hid it in Marty Leigh's latest mystery novel, replacing the bookmark.

♥ ♥ ♥

Sunday, the next day, was both strange and sweet. Danny *and* Jared expected me to sit with them in Sunday school. And on the chair right between them, no less. Paula and Kayla snickered into their Bibles, while Stan shot Andie a knowing look.

It was a good thing Andrew Barnett was nowhere in sight. He'd think I was just another silly eighth grader, trying to juggle more than one guy friend at a time. I was poised first on one edge of my chair, and then the other, depending on how far Danny or Jared leaned at any given moment, trying to keep my arms from touching either of them. Most girls would have been flattered having two cute guys after them, but not me. My sights were set on one, and only one, mature true love.

♥   ♥   ♥

Monday came at last and, lucky for me, Paula was working as a student-aide in the office before school. I was in a big hurry, as usual. Motioning her over, I whispered my intentions. "Can you put this in Mr. Barnett's box for me?"

Her eyes brightened. "What's this about?"

"I'll tell you at lunch."

She took the envelope, and I turned around. Holding my breath, I waited outside the office. When I was sure she'd had time to sneak off to the faculty mail area, I peeked my head around the doorway. She grinned at me. It was the only sign I needed.

Feeling mighty smug, as well as eager for Andrew's response, I sailed off toward my locker.

Jared was waiting.

"You're not going to sing to me today, are you?" I teased.

"How about we practice our duet, you know the one—'Something Good'?" He leaned against the locker door.

"Oh no, you don't," I said, pushing him away. That song was supposed to end with a long kiss. At least, that's how it was in the movie. We still didn't know what Mr. Barnett wanted us to do there. And I wasn't about to ask.

"You're not worried about that scene, are you?" he asked, a frown of kindness on his face.

"I, uh, guess not."

He pushed his hands into his jeans pockets. "Funny, isn't it?"

There was an awkward silence.

"What's funny?" I said.

"There just aren't enough girls like you to go around, Holly-Heart." There was a sober ring to his voice.

I broke the spell. "Don't be weird." I found my books for science and closed my locker.

"I mean it." He fell in step with me as I headed to first period. "Danny thinks so, too."

Oh great, I thought. Now they were conferring with each other about me.

"C'mon, Holly. Don't be mad. I mean, what's a guy to do? We can't ignore you."

"You could try." I waved him on as I opened the

door to Mr. Ross's class, thinking only of the note I'd written to Mr. Barnett. And his response to it. What would it be?

♥   ♥   ♥

After school, we met for play practice. Today we were going to work through the speaking parts onstage. Excited and very nervous, I hurried into the auditorium.

Danny and his stage crew sat on the edge of the stage, waiting for instructions from Miss Hess and Mr. Barnett. I sat between Paula and Andie, hoping to escape Jared's attention, but he squeezed in next to me, making Andie slide over.

Mr. Barnett passed out a rehearsal schedule. I glanced over it, wondering how I'd ever survive the next few weeks. While he gave instructions for blocking, I wondered if he'd checked his mailbox yet, or read my note. If he had, he wasn't letting on. Not by a secret smile or even a special look. The real truth was he probably hadn't had a chance to check.

"Okay, let's start with act one, skip to scenes two and three," he said, cupping his hand over his mouth to amplify his voice. "Everyone pretend we're in the Nonnberg Abbey, back in the thirties, in Salzburg, Austria."

Andie, Kayla, Joy, and Shauna took their places in the imaginary abbey, pretending to be solemn and nunlike. Andie's face was so solemn it was actually funny as she took her place behind the Reverend Mother's desk.

My throat felt dry as I took my place onstage. In the scene, Maria had just come in from singing and frolicking in the hills of Austria when the Mother Abbess calls her into her office for a chat.

Things went well with that scene. Andie behaved herself, trying to act holier than anyone onstage. It was a kick. She actually folded her hands and walked around looking rather stuffy.

When it came time for me to meet Captain von Trapp in the great hall at the von Trapp villa, I kept spotting a nose and a pair of eyes peeking through the curtains in front of me. Very distracting. I motioned to the person, whoever it was, to close the curtain. "Go away," I whispered while Jared said his lines. It was in the middle of the captain's dialogue, where he instructs me how to call his seven children with a whistle.

Suddenly Mr. Barnett came up onstage. "Holly?"

"Yes?" I answered, glancing at his shirt pocket, wondering if my note had been tucked away for safe-keeping.

"Are you practicing lines while Jared is speaking?"

"Oh no. It's that." I pointed to the gap in the curtains. Quickly, they sprang shut.

"Carry on," Mr. Barnett instructed. And we did.

Later, during the romantic scene between Maria and Captain von Trapp, the nose and eyes appeared through the curtains again. This time, a wisp of auburn hair showed, as well. The hair gave him away. It was Danny, spying on scenes. Scenes where Jared's and my character were supposed to be romantically involved.

After practice, I located Danny backstage. "Have fun snooping today?"

He ignored me, shuffling around with props and things.

"You really could be watching from the audience," I suggested. "Why'd you take this stage manager job, anyway, if you're just going to gawk?"

He shook his head innocently, but I was sure I knew the answer. Finally he left, and I was searching for my script when I overheard Miss Hess and Mr. Barnett talking together.

"You could've signed your name," he was saying to her.

"I'm not sure what you're talking about," Miss Hess answered coyly.

I held my breath as I eavesdropped backstage.

His smile gave way to a grin. "Oh, you can deny

it, but I'm telling you it was a nice surprise."

I peeked through the curtain as he continued. "I think we ought to discuss things further over coffee, or is tea better for you?"

I nearly choked. Andrew was totally mixed up. He thought Miss Hess had written the anonymous note—*my* note. It was all I could do to keep from leaping through the curtains and setting the record straight.

As Mr. Barnett planned their rendezvous for tomorrow after school at the Soda Straw, Miss Hess smiled back at him, obviously delighted. There she stood, just outside the orchestra pit, letting him think whatever he wanted. Letting my note do the job she'd probably hoped to arrange all along!

I gripped the folds of the curtain. End of act two, scene two. So much for my crazy little scheme. The curtain had come crashing down around me, without any applause.

I waited, watching as they left the auditorium together. The custodian came in to turn out the lights before I could muster the strength to come out and face the empty chairs. People or no people, there would be a grand musical here, and I was Maria, the star of the show. Mr. Barnett had thought I was the best choice for the lead. He'd said I was the perfect Maria.

Was that all I was? Just a talented drama student? With a heavy heart, I trudged down the steps and walked the long aisle to the back doors, replaying the conversation in his car.

What was all his talk about age differences? Was he simply toying with my heart? Or was he actually referring to Miss Hess?

Andie and Paula waited for me at the bus stop. Running to meet them, I nearly tripped, but I caught myself.

"Watch out," Paula called.

"I'm okay," I said. And I was—on the outside. Inside I was a wreck.

The bus arrived and its door screeched open.

"Good practice today," Andie said, jostling for a seat in the back of the bus. She and I sat together. Paula sat in front of us, saving a place for her twin, who was running down the street, frantically flagging the driver.

Andie giggled. "Look at Kayla go."

"You should see her jog around the courthouse," I said. "You too, Paula. You guys are fast." It almost made me wish I'd gone out for track instead of the musical.

"You look terrible, Holly," Andie offered.

"Thanks, I needed that."

Paula turned around just as an exhausted Kayla slumped into the seat next to her. "Holly, you okay?"

I sighed. "The note I sent Mr. Barnett backfired," I said, feeling more foolish than ever. "Guess I should've signed my name."

"Are you crazy?" Andie said. "No way!"

"What happened?" Paula asked.

I told them the conversation I'd witnessed between Miss Hess and Mr. Barnett.

"You're kidding." Kayla turned around, suddenly coming to life. "Miss Hess likes Mr. Barnett?"

"Sure seems like it," I said. "Now what should I do?" I felt like crying.

"You could always write another note," Paula suggested. "Just tell him you wrote the first one and sign your name this time."

"No, no!" Andie was emphatic. "Holly can't be stupid about this. There's a better way."

"If he really does like me, like he said on Saturday, then what's to lose?" I said. "Why couldn't I write him another letter?"

"Wait a minute," Andie said. "Try to remember everything he said on Saturday."

What was she getting at?

Andie took a deep breath. "Here's the deal. If there's the slightest chance that Mr. Barnett was thinking about Miss Hess, or some other older woman, you've simply misread him. But if he was actually talking about you and him, well . . . that's what we've gotta find out."

"And as soon as possible," I said. "Or else Miss Hess could move in on him and I'd lose my chance for true love."

"Oh, please," Andie blurted, rolling her eyes at me.

"You might have another problem," Paula said. "What if he *is* interested in you, and he's not a Christian. What then?"

"Yeah," Andie sighed. "You know the verse in the Bible about not being yoked together with unbelievers. Besides, your mom won't let you date till you're fifteen anyway. He'd have to wait a whole year."

"I know," I said, trying to ignore that fact.

"Do you think he'll wait for you if it turns out he's . . . well, you know, in love with you?" Paula asked.

"Why not?" I said. "The way I see it, he'd have a chance to finish his degree and get settled into a good teaching position, maybe even here in Dressel Hills."

Kayla giggled. "Looks like you've got it all worked out . . . in your head."

"Wait a minute," Andie said, looking serious. "When's your article coming out?"

Kayla gasped. "You mean she interviewed Mr. Barnett for the school paper?"

Andie nodded slowly. "You betcha. This girl doesn't waste time. When's it coming out?" she repeated.

I said, "Next week, I think."

"That's good," said Andie excitedly. "Because when it's out, here's what you do. You take your copy to Mr. Barnett and ask him to sign it. You know, get his autograph, since he'll be leaving at the end of the school year."

I groaned. "What'll *that* do?"

"Hold on a minute," Andie said as Paula and Kayla looked on, wide-eyed. "It'll give you a chance to talk with him again—one on one. We'll even guard the choir room doors, won't we, girls?"

The Miller twins nodded in sync.

"Sounds ridiculous," I said, thinking I was in way over my head.

Andie got huffy suddenly. "Well, Holly, if you don't like that, you could always try the direct approach. Just blurt it out—ask him what he meant by all that age stuff."

"Now, *there's* a thought," I whispered sarcastically. But I had a better plan. One I wasn't going to reveal. Not in a zillion years.

When Downhill Court came up, I prepared to exit through the back door of the bus. I could see that Andie was over the worst. She was talking a mile a minute to the Miller twins. That's how she was. Mad one minute, best friends the next.

"See ya," I called to them.

"Call me," Paula said.

"Me too," Andie said.

"See you tomorrow." I stepped off the bus and headed across the street, intercepting the mail truck. I waited for the mail carrier to sort our mail, noticing Daddy's handwriting on one of the envelopes. Feeling guilty about not responding to his good news earlier, I hurried into the house with the mail.

Uncle Jack and the younger boys were doing math at the dining room table. Uncle Jack looked up as I came in. "Late practice?" he asked.

"It'll be this way from now till opening night." I handed the mail to him but kept the letter addressed to me from California.

He spotted the envelope in my hand. "I hear your dad recently became a Christian."

"Uh-huh."

"That's terrific," he said, running his fingers through the top of his hair. "I've been praying for him since before I married his sister, back twenty years ago."

"Wow," Phil said. "That's a long time."

"You're not joking," Mark piped up. "I prayed for a boy at school, you know, back in Pennsylvania, and he just got worse."

"But you didn't give up, did you?" Phil asked soberly.

"Not really, but I got tired of being bullied. I prayed the Lord would make him move away or turn him into a Christian." Mark bit the eraser on his pencil.

"What happened?" I asked.

"God didn't answer either of my prayers, but He did do something else."

Uncle Jack grinned like he knew the answer.

"God moved us out here." Mark blinked his eyes, smiling.

"Our Lord works in mysterious ways," Uncle Jack said. "Right, kiddo?" He looked at me. And somehow I felt he understood my struggle about my father becoming a Christian.

"People are mysterious, too, sometimes," I muttered, heading for the stairs. What I really meant to say was: Why did Daddy's decision for Christ upset me so much? It was wrong for me to hang on to something that had happened six years ago.

In my room, I sat on my window seat, letting Goofey curl up beside me. Slowly, almost fearfully, I opened the letter from sunny California.

13

Daddy's letter was full of church-related activities; he was attending a businessmen's prayer breakfast every Saturday. He didn't comment about the fact that I hadn't answered his last letter, but he'd heard about our school musical and that I had been chosen to play Maria. The news of the musical had come from Grandma Meredith, his mother, who still kept in close contact with Mom. In fact, Mom talked on the phone with her several times a month. She and Grandpa had always said we were still their family in spite of the divorce. And now even more so, since Mom had married their former son-in-law, Uncle Jack.

I held the letter in my hands, letting the late afternoon sun beat on it. Tears filled my eyes as I remembered the years of my prayers for Daddy. The man who'd abandoned us six years ago. God had forgiven him; so should I. But when I prayed, I could only say, "Thank you, Lord, for answering my prayers about Daddy." The forgiving part would have to come later. If at all.

Picking up Goofey, I gave him a hug. "It's time to invite someone very special to come see *The Sound of Music*, junior-high style," I told my cat.

Goofey began licking his paws, giving himself a bath on the sun-dappled window seat. I went to my desk, pulled out some plain stationery, and began writing.

When I finished, I read the letter. "Daddy probably won't come, you know," I said over my shoulder to Goofey, who was now sound asleep. "He's too busy with his work. That's how it's always been. But at least he knows I want him to come."

I added a *P.S.* to the letter. *I'm up to my eyelids in scripts and rehearsals. That's why I haven't written.*

On my way to the bus stop the next morning, I walked to the mailbox to mail my letter, wishing with all my heart he'd arrange his schedule and come see the performance. But knowing Daddy, I wouldn't hold my breath.

By fourth period, Andie had heard some strange rumors about Jared and me. "Everyone's talking about the romantic scene in the play," she said. "I've heard that Jared plans to kiss you for real."

"Just let him try," I said, boiling mad.

Andie giggled. "C'mon, Holly, it's not like you haven't thought about what it would be like."

"That was then, this is now." I was thinking about the months he and I were going together . . . sorta.

"Maybe today's the day to talk to Mr. Barnett about what he wants you guys to do." She lowered her voice to a whisper as we walked into the choir room with a bunch of other kids. "Maybe he'll say just fake the kiss, but watch his face when he tells you."

"How come?"

"Think about it, Holly," Andie insisted. "It'll give you some insight, you know, into how he might feel about you."

"Oh," I said. Once again, Andie was on top of things.

After class, Andie nudged me. "Don't forget to watch his face, especially his eyes. You can tell how someone feels by their eyes."

"Okay, okay." I waited till the choir room was empty. Andie left just before I approached Mr. Barnett's desk.

"Ah, it's you, Maria herself," he greeted me warmly.

"I've been thinking," I began. "That scene outside, beside the gazebo, uh, where Captain von Trapp proposes to Maria, what should Jared and I do there?"

He looked down, twiddling his pen. "That's a good question." He leaned back in his chair, looking me straight in the eye. "How do you feel about it?"

Not fair! I wanted *him* to tell *me*.

Mr. Barnett stood up. "You know, Holly, you could talk it over with the leading man."

"But what do *you* think we should do?" There, the ball was back in his court.

"Well, to tell you the truth, my feeling is to leave out the kiss and just fake it. But make it look real. Okay with you?"

I was relieved. Could he see it in my eyes?

"Thanks, Mr. Barnett, I'll tell Jared what you said." I turned to leave.

"Oh, Holly, before you leave, I've been wanting to talk to you."

"Yes?" I was hyperventilating for sure. What was he going to say?

"It's about your church," he said. "I was impressed with the kids from your youth group last Saturday."

"Thanks," I said, not sure how to respond.

"I've been looking for a good church. Maybe I'll visit yours sometime. Do you go to the early or late service?"

"Usually the early," I said, barely able to get the words out.

"Good." He smiled warmly. "I'll see you there."

I scurried out of the choir room and off to lunch, my heart in my throat. Wait'll Andie heard *this*!

♥ ♥ ♥

Backstage that afternoon, things were crowded. I found Jared ready to go with script in hand. It was the day to rehearse the romantic scene.

"We have to talk," I said, pointing him to a quiet corner near the makeshift dressing rooms.

He looked worried. "Everything okay?"

"I talked to Mr. Barnett today about this scene."

"Yeah?" He seemed concerned.

"He wants us to leave off the kiss." I said it firmly, without hesitation.

He looked a little disappointed. "Whatever you want to do is fine."

I couldn't believe my ears. I honestly thought he'd fight for the kiss.

Later, during the actual scene, Jared seemed distant. No, guarded. Like he didn't want to offend me or something.

Mr. Barnett stopped us. "Jared, you're going through the motions. Think about this moment," he said. "You're declaring your love to Maria." He glanced at me. "The captain's been a lonely man since his wife died years ago, and all these children . . . think of trying to raise seven kids by yourself. Now, can you warm up to this pretty Maria of yours a little more?"

Mr. Barnett stepped back while Jared said his lines again.

"Still not enough feeling," Mr. Barnett interrupted. He pulled Jared off to the side. "Look, have you ever been in love?"

"I think so," Jared said, glancing at me.

"Well, terrific," Mr. Barnett said, clapping his hands. "Can you transfer those feelings to Holly here, er, Maria? Isn't she lovely? Don't you want to let her know how much she means to you? She's going to be your wife, for pete's sake!"

That did it. Jared warmed up, all right. Too much. I could see the love practically oozing from his eyes.

Finally Mr. Barnett was delighted with our performance. He called it quits earlier than usual, probably because he had that date scheduled with Miss Hess.

I fooled around backstage, making sure everyone was gone before I made my move. Then I snuck into the props room to set the wheels of my perfect plan in motion. First, I found Andie's Mother Abbess habit, complete with robe and wimple. Then I located some pillows to fill me out a bit. I shivered with excitement as I slipped into the habit and looked at myself in the mirror. Fabulous! No one would ever know it was me.

With another quick glance at the mirror, I was off to the Soda Straw to spy on Mr. Barnett and Miss Hess.

I couldn't remember ever having seen Catholic nuns in the Dressel Hills area, but I guess there was always a first time. Solemnly, deliberately, I made my way out the backstage door, hoping to bypass teachers and other students. Most everyone had gone home for the day, so I didn't see a single soul as I took short, reverent steps to the Soda Straw.

I pushed the door open gently, wishing the jingling bell didn't have to sound every time someone entered. And there they were—Mr. Barnett and Miss Hess, looking too cozy together in a corner booth. They never even turned around when the bell jingled. A bad sign. A sign that they were too deeply involved in conversation to care.

I chose the booth next to them, careful to sit with my back to Mr. Barnett. I wanted to hear *his* remarks.

The waitress came around, smiling politely.

"What can I get for you today, Sister?"

I glanced at the menu and saw precisely what I wanted. "This looks good," I said, disguising my voice.

"A banana split?" She seemed surprised. Had I done something wrong? Something out of character for a righteous woman?

"Yes, please," I said. "With extra strawberries and whipped cream, if you don't mind."

She jotted down the order and scurried off. I stared at the stools lined up at the aluminum counter as I eavesdropped on the conversation directly behind me. So far it was rather boring. Nothing like the ear-tingling things Mr. Barnett and I had discussed last Saturday. Or before that, in the choir room, the day he played his composition for me.

"Teaching on the junior high level is very challenging, but I have to admit that I do enjoy it," Miss Hess was saying.

"So far, it's fun," Mr. Barnett agreed. "But what I'd really like to do is get my doctorate and teach at the college level."

"What about coaching drama?" she asked. "You're so good at it."

There was a slight pause. "I've been involved with summer stock since high school," Mr. Barnett said. "But it's very different coming from the other side of the orchestra pit, if you know what I mean."

Miss Hess sighed. "Getting students to loosen up onstage takes some doing. Especially young teens."

The waitress came back with my banana split with strawberries and extra whipped cream. "Here you are, Sister."

I nodded, smiling, relinquishing the opportunity to speak. The less I used my vocal chords, disguised or otherwise, the safer I would be.

My ears perked up when I heard my name in the booth behind me. "Holly sure has a feel for the stage," Mr. Barnett said. "Has she had parts in other plays at school?"

Miss Hess said, "I think this is her first play. But her composition teacher says she has a vivid imagination and does quite a lot of writing."

Mr. Barnett chuckled. "She sure knows how to conduct a good interview. I can't wait to see what she wrote about me in the school paper."

Suddenly Miss Hess changed the subject. Was she jealous?

"How long have you lived in Colorado?" she asked.

"My folks moved here from Seattle when I was a kid," Mr. Barnett said. "What about you?"

Boring small talk.

"I'm one of the few natives around," Miss Hess said, almost boastfully. "Ask me anything about Colorado—its music, its culture—"

"Its anonymous letter writers?" Mr. Barnett interrupted.

I almost choked on a banana. No, not that!

Miss Hess actually giggled. *Now* she was enjoying the conversation.

"I didn't write that note to you, Andrew. Honest."

Would he believe her this time?

"C'mon, Vickie," he said. "Tell the truth."

It sounded like he wished she *had* written the note!

"I told you," she said coyly.

"Are you sure about this?"

I could almost see the mischievous twinkle in his eye. Why wouldn't he listen to Miss Hess?

Confused, I spooned up a bite of ice cream. It sure seemed like Mr. Barnett was flirting with Miss Hess. He even called her Vickie! Was he just a fun-loving tease?

I thought about his other wonderful words. *"Holly sure has a feel for the stage . . . she knows how to conduct a good interview. . . ."*

I heard Miss Hess talking again. "Looks like you have a thing for pistachio."

Although I didn't dare turn around, I could visualize a mountain of pistachio ice cream.

Mr. Barnett chuckled softly. "One thing's for sure. The woman I marry better not mind a few pistachio shells around the house."

The woman? Where did that leave me?

The door jingled, and Andie and Paula waltzed in with Stan and Billy Hill. Yikes!

I flew off to the ladies' room. Not very holylike, but, oh well.

Inside one of the stalls, I undressed, thankful I'd left my own clothes on underneath. *Love does strange things to people,* I thought, trying to figure out how to smuggle Andie's costume out of here.

Just then, Andie flew into the rest room. "Holly," she called to me in the stall.

I waited silently. Without breathing.

"I know you're in here," she continued. "And I saw you in that nun's habit. What on earth are you doing parading around in my costume?"

I tried to stifle the giggles, but it was no use. They came pouring out, a little at first, then out came a full-fledged burst.

"You're so-o immature," Andie said. "Now come out here and talk to me."

Slowly, I emerged from the bathroom stall. "How'd you know it was me?"

"How'd I know?" She nearly collapsed with laughter. "You left your hair hanging out, that's how! Your hair's a good three inches longer than the wimple, you know."

I gasped. "Really? Oh, Andie, this is horrible. What if Mr. Barnett saw it, too?"

She shook her head, raising her eyebrows. "Why

didn't you tell me what you were doing? I could've advised you . . . helped you."

"You still can," I pleaded. "Get your school bag or your purse. Anything." I began folding the habit.

"I don't have anything with me that'll hold the costume," she said.

"Just please try." I stood there holding the costume and looking in the mirror at my hair as she left. How stupid of me! Why hadn't I taken time to plan this more carefully?

Andie said to wait here—"I'll be right back!"

And she was. She flew in the door, and we began to stuff the habit into her school bag. Then, attempting to hide the bulging evidence, we returned to the booth where Paula, Billy, and Stan were waiting to order.

I slid in next to Paula. Glancing over at Mr. Barnett and Miss Hess, I hoped they hadn't noticed my blond hair earlier. Then I spotted my perfectly good banana split waiting to be devoured. My heart sank. Which was worse? Wasting a delicious dessert or making a total fool of myself?

Shortly, Mr. Barnett and Miss Hess left via the jingling door. I dashed back to my table, rescuing my banana split just as the waitress came to remove it. She wore a vague, puzzled look as I told her, "Don't worry. I'll pay for it. The Sister won't be back."

At least, not if I could help it.

I ate the remains of my sweet treat, rethinking my amateur spying attempts. While Billy and Paula bantered back and forth, I came to this realization: I was not nearly as mature as I'd thought. The truth was, I'd made a major blunder, forgetting to hide my hair under the wimple.

Two days later, on Friday, I was still trying to live it down. At least with Paula and Andie.

"You don't have to be perfect to be mature," Andie said, waiting at my locker for Paula. They were coming for a sleepover at my house.

"I know, but it's so humiliating." I closed my locker door.

"What about Mr. Barnett?" Andie asked. "Do you think he saw your hair hanging out?"

"Nah, I can tell by the way he acts around me."

Andie waved as Paula came down the hall. Then, turning to me, she said, "I'm so glad you're having us over. It'll be so cool practicing our lines together. Maybe we can get one of your younger brothers to read the guys' lines."

"Don't forget, Stan'll be hanging around," I said. "He might fill in some of the parts for us."

"Just so he and Paula don't get any ideas and rehearse that romantic scene of theirs," Andie snapped.

When we arrived at my house, Mom was tossing a gigantic salad and putting the finishing touches on a homemade pizza. Leave it to Mom to make the perfect food for a party.

After supper, we headed for my room, scripts in hand. Since Stan was busy with Phil and Mark, playing the final level on a hold-your-breath computer game, I suggested we take turns filling in the parts of the male leads. Things went smoothly for over an hour, but soon our dry throats were ready for something cold and soothing. Mom offered to make root beer floats, and she brought them up to us on a tray.

Handing me a frosty-cold glass, she said, "Holly, your father called this morning. He's coming to Dressel Hills . . . for your play."

"He is?" I gasped. "Oh no, hand me my script."

I caught it as Andie tossed it to me.

After Mom left, we started all over again on Act One. After two more times through, we stopped practicing lines and shared secrets. Secrets about crushes on older guys. Especially the adult variety. Andie got it started by recounting the hilarious scene at the Soda Straw. She went to my closet and pulled out a yellow sweater and tucked it inside her oversized T-shirt. Marching around the room, Andie took ladylike steps, the way Mr. Barnett had instructed her to as the Mother Abbess. Paula and I laughed hysterically as the long yellow sleeve dangled down her back—the way my long hair had under the nun's wimple.

"It's not very funny, when you think about it," Paula said, recovering from giggling. "I remember having a huge crush on a teacher back east, before we ever moved here."

Andie stopped cold. "Really?" She looked horrified, then began to laugh.

"It happens," I said, eager to plan my next move with Mr. Barnett. It was time to come forward and let him know how I felt.

Andie quit laughing and pulled my sweater down out of her top. She lowered her voice and checked the door. "Huddle up," she whispered.

By the look in Andie's eyes, I knew this was going to be good. Secrets were dancing in the air tonight.

"Promise not to tell anyone?" she began.

Paula and I nodded.

"Not a soul?" she demanded.

"You've got my word," Paula said.

"Ditto for me," I said.

Andie leaned in close to us on the floor. She opened her mouth to speak. Then she caught herself.

"Quick, Holly. Turn on your radio," she said.

I frowned. "What's the secret?"

"Hurry," Andie insisted. "We need music to drown this out."

I did as she asked, finding a contemporary Christian music station. "How's that?"

She nodded as I scurried back to my place like a mouse hungry for a morsel of cheese.

When our heads were close enough to tell who'd brushed teeth after pizza and who hadn't, Andie began. "Remember when Pastor Rob first came to Dressel Hills?"

I remembered. Andie and I were only eleven.

"Well," she continued, "I had this enormous crush on him. It was like every time I saw him at church, I fell in love all over again. I can't believe I ran around asking to help him with church stuff. He must've known. Especially after I told him I'd put his name at the top of my prayer list."

I gasped. "You *told* him that?"

"Give me a break." She grinned broadly. "I was in fifth grade back then."

"How come you never told me?" I asked.

"Because I thought you liked him, too."

I grinned. "I did, but I didn't want you to know."

"This sounds like true confessions night," Paula said.

"Yeah, right," I said, thinking of Mr. Barnett.

♥ ♥ ♥

The next day, after the girls' parents picked them up, I hopped on my bike and rode downtown. I now had the perfect plan—with pistachio nuts at the center of it. Mr. Barnett had a weakness for pistachios; he'd said it himself.

I locked up my bike in front of Explore Bookstore and hurried a few stores down to the drugstore. Every kind of nut imaginable could be found in large bins. Locating the pistachio variety, I told the clerk I wanted enough to fill the plastic container on display.

"One moment, please." And he disappeared behind the counter.

Soon, I was the proud owner of two pounds of pistachio nuts, the perfect answer to my dilemma. I couldn't wait to present them to Mr. Barnett on Monday.

♥ ♥ ♥

Sunday—*gasp!*—he showed up at my church wearing a sharp, double-breasted dark suit and maroon-and-white tie. Since I'd never seen him dressed up that much, I nearly fainted on the spot.

Andie spotted him, too. "Would you look at that," she said, gawking at him across the foyer.

"Quiet," I whispered.

"He's come to take you away," she teased.

"Go sit with your mother," I insisted.

"See ya." And she turned and headed toward the inside doors, with a quick glance back at me.

Just as I was reaching for the church bulletin, Mr. Barnett came up to me. "Good morning, Holly. What's on the program for today?"

Program? Was he for real?

I shuffled through the bulletin, aware of my increasing anxiety—maybe because Mr. Barnett was standing so close. "Here. It looks like our senior pastor is speaking. You'll like him," I said, smiling.

Mr. Barnett hesitated slightly. Then he said, "I thought I'd sit with Stan if he won't mind."

"No problem. Follow me," I said, giddier than ever. I led him down the aisle, to our family's pew. Stan was sitting on the end. I poked him. "Hey, cuz."

He looked up.

"Mr. Barnett is visiting our church, and he'd like some company," I whispered, gesturing toward our teacher.

Stan smiled and said hello to Mr. Barnett, then slid over to make room. Thank goodness he wasn't making a big deal of this.

I caught Andie's glance across the church as I sat down at the end of the pew—next to Andrew Barnett. I wasn't sure, but it looked like—for once—she was close to fainting.

♥ ♥ ♥

If sitting in church on a springtime Sunday with the main focus of my affection wasn't enough, on Monday during choir he asked me to stay after class. He needed to see me about something. Fabulous! Maybe that would be a good time to give him my gift.

Gingerly, I set my school bag down on the riser as we warmed up for sectionals. Neither Andie nor Paula asked about the obvious bulge. My Pistachio Plan was perfect, and in just fifty minutes, Mr. Barnett would know the truth.

After class, Mr. Barnett had a question about my style preference for a wedding gown. For the wedding scene in the musical, of course.

"Footloose and Fancy Things has some fabulous gowns," I said. "In fact, they might loan one to the school just for the play."

"In exchange for free advertising, perhaps," he said. "Good thinking, Holly."

Billy Hill and some other boys stood at the door just as I was about to present my gift. Mr. Barnett went over to them; his back was turned to me.

Without hesitation, I pulled out the plastic container filled with his favorite kind of nuts. I glanced at the gift card I'd found for him at Explore Bookstore. It was signed: *Love, H*. Gently, I placed the nut-filled bowl on his desk.

The door closed and Mr. Barnett came smiling back to me. "What's this?" he asked, obviously delighted.

"I, uh . . . I brought this for you." Butterflies played tag in my stomach.

"Incredible." He reached for the card.

For a moment, I waited, dying for his reaction.

When he had read the card, he glanced up, grinning. "That Miss Hess! Did she put you up to this?"

"I . . . er, I—" It was hopeless, the words were stuck. And this might be my last chance to tell him, face-to-face, how I felt.

For what seemed like a never-ending moment, we just looked at each other. Then suddenly the intercom crackled. "Mr. Barnett, you have a phone call, can you take it in the office?"

He turned to face the speaker high on the wall. "I'll be right down." Then, beaming at me, he said,

"Thanks for taking time to play delivery girl. You're really very sweet."

After he left, I stood there, stunned. Staring at the Pistachio Plan—make that Total Flop—on his desk, I felt numb. Sick.

Not again!

The next four weeks were a total nightmare. Everywhere I turned, Mr. Barnett was there. At practice every day. In my dreams at night. And, as before, in my daydreams. But I didn't dare make an attempt to tell him how I felt. Not after two plans had so totally failed. I'd be testing fate to try again.

To make matters worse, the practice schedule escalated to every day after school and three evenings a week! Lines had been memorized, but now came the emphasis on facial expressions and body movements. Mr. Barnett got right in there and worked us through all the important inflections.

Character dynamics were essential, too. Stephie, my stepsister, was a superb little Marta—my youngest charge as the governess, Maria. Our interaction onstage reflected the close relationship we had at home. Same with Stan. Andie, Paula, and I were close friends, so working together onstage was a cinch for us, too.

With the constant practicing, Jared and I were actually developing a good working relationship, too. And offstage, he hardly ever flirted with me. Well, not severely, at least.

As for Mr. Barnett, I couldn't summon the courage to tell him the truth about the pistachio nuts, but it was obvious by the trail of shells on his desk that he was enjoying them.

♥　♥　♥

Finally it was the afternoon of May 27: dress rehearsal. We performed in front of the elementary school down the street from my house. Carrie and our stepbrothers, Phil and Mark, sat in the audience with their respective classes. From their talk at breakfast that morning, I knew they were as excited as Stephie and I.

I peeked through the curtains, looking for my brothers and sister, hoping to dazzle them and their friends with my rendition of Maria. More than anything, though, I intended to impress Mr. Barnett.

At the end of each scene, the kids clapped loudly. They seemed to like Jared's introduction of his children with his weird whistle calls. But Jared had seemed a little out of it. And his face looked awfully pale.

Backstage, before final curtain calls, Mr. Barnett said this was our best performance yet. "Now tonight, keep your audience in mind as you say your lines." He was a stickler for enunciation. "If they can't understand you, we're toast."

Danny nodded. He ought to know, after the tons of eavesdropping he'd been doing on our performances. Guess that's the way it had to be as stage manager, though. Knowing who was where and what was what. He was good.

Still, I had eyes for only one person. And as Mr. Barnett talked, I longed for a way to share my true feelings. A foolproof way—one that wouldn't flop.

♥   ♥   ♥

After a quick taco salad for supper, Mom flew around the house getting Stephie ready for our big production.

"I'm really scared," Stephie said.

"You'll be fine," I said, squeezing her around the waist.

Carrie helped Stephie carry her things to the van. The rest of the family planned to come later, in time for the best seats.

When I arrived at the dressing room, Andie was all aflutter. "What if I forget my lines?" she worried.

"It'll never happen," I said. "You think so fast on your feet, Andie, you could make it up if you forget."

"How's it feel getting married to Jared onstage in front of everyone?" Paula asked with a grin.

"You would ask that," I said. "How's it feel kissing my cousin?" I thought about Stan and Paula onstage as the love struck couple, Liesl and Rolf.

Andie jerked away from the mirror, horrified. "Who's kissing?"

Paula giggled. "Don't worry, Andie, we're only faking it."

"Yeah, well, don't get too close." She wasn't kidding.

"Don't worry," Paula said. "Billy, the butler, asked to take me to the cast party tomorrow night."

I leaped up, hugging her. "Really? You and Billy, at last?"

Andie smiled. "You'll like him. We went out for a while last year, before Stan moved here."

"Hello?" someone called through the dressing-room curtain.

I looked around. "Everyone decent?"

"Go for it," Andie called.

I moved back the curtain, poking my head out. And there he stood, looking absolutely fabulous in his tan business suit—even the silk hankie matched his tie. "Daddy!" I cried, letting the curtain go as we hugged.

"This is your big night, Holly," he whispered. "I couldn't miss it for the world, could I?"

I grinned with excitement. "I can't wait till you see the show!"

"Well, the place is filling up fast," he said. "I'll be praying for you."

"Thanks, I need it."

He held my hand, and for a moment I thought of the pain he'd caused our family. The lousy way he'd treated Mom . . .

His eyes searched mine. "What is it, honey?"

Instead of launching my questions, probing into the pain of the past, I reached out and hugged him again. Bone-hard, like Mom hugs me sometimes. "I love you, Daddy," I whispered. "That's all. Just . . . I love you."

In his arms, the need to confront him disappeared, and my heart overflowed with forgiveness and joy for his newfound faith in God. Slowly, I pulled away. "I'd better get my makeup on."

"Break a leg, Holly-Heart." Smile lines creased his face.

"Thanks."

♥　♥　♥

The musical might have been called *The Flight*

of the Butterflies the way my stomach flip-flopped before curtains. Packed to capacity, the auditorium was a sellout. And to think my father had come all the way from California to see me!

My hands felt damp and my heart pounded as I listened to the buzz of the crowd. If only Gabriel would blow his trumpet right now.

Then the overture began, with gentle woodwinds setting the mood, followed by the fuller sound of strings. The joyous melody swelled to a crescendo, soothing me. As I took my place onstage, waiting for the rush of rising curtains, I sent up a silent prayer.

Act one, scene one, the hills of Austria. Exhilarated by the excitement of the crowd, I spun around at center stage, swinging my arms wide and singing the theme song, "The Sound of Music."

Mr. Barnett watched from the orchestra pit. His face, the way it shone in the stage lights, spurred me on to greater heights. *Oh, if only I could tell him my true feelings before he leaves*, I thought as the orchestra played my interlude. Time was running out. Student teachers don't stick around forever. School would soon be out for the year. How could I pull it off?

The audience applauded as I sang the reprise, then the curtain fell, ending the first scene. I ran into the wings, awaiting my next cue.

But, just then, a commotion broke out backstage. Andie grabbed my arm. "Jared's real sick; he's going home," she said.

"He's what?" I rushed to the chair where he sat with his head down. Leaning over, I placed my hand on his shoulder. "Jared, are you okay?"

He looked at me momentarily. A weak smile flitted across his deathly white face. "I'm sorry to let you down like this, Maria, my love."

It was the sweetest thing he'd ever said. On or offstage.

Suddenly Mr. Barnett showed up. "What happened?"

"He's been throwing up," Andie explained while Paula and Kayla and all the others looked on.

Jared moaned. "I nearly blacked out."

Quickly, Mr. Barnett turned to Andie and me. "You girls go ahead with the next two scenes. The captain isn't on till scene four."

Andie and I hurried for the stage, passing Danny in the wings. "The walking microchip could play your leading man," Andie whispered in my ear.

"He knows the lines all right," I agreed. But we both knew he could never pull it off. Besides, no one could run ship behind the curtains as well as Danny.

Worried about Jared, I took my place onstage, and the curtains rose slowly. It was hard to concentrate on my lines with the part of Captain up for grabs.

At the tail end of scene three, the music swelled

as I headed for the von Trapp villa—eager, yet worried about the job of being governess for seven children. But I was *more* worried about my leading man, sick and trembling, backstage.

The audience clapped as the curtains fell again. Dashing backstage, I found the janitor cleaning up the floor near Jared's chair. I didn't have to ask why.

"His parents took him home," Stan said solemnly.

"So, now what?"

Stan stood up. "Better ask Mr. Barnett."

Danny motioned to me from the wings. "Take your position, Maria," he whispered. His flashlight led me to the floor marks. Next came Billy as Franz, the butler.

Not knowing who would play the male lead, I waited, jittery and tense. Next to passing out at the seventh-grade musical, having my leading man get sick was the next worst thing. I felt sorry for Jared, missing his opening night. But I was also sorry for myself, and possibly the audience, depending on who was appointed the role of Captain von Trapp.

Then, suddenly Mr. Barnett strolled onstage. Wearing a navy blue sea captain's uniform, he was as handsome as ever. Danny pointed with his flashlight to an easy chair on stage left. And the new Captain von Trapp sat down.

Mr. Barnett smiled. In the semidarkness my heart danced off beat. And together, we waited for curtains.

I remembered Miss W's words the day she'd described how to create an element of surprise during creative writing class. *By bringing two unrelated entities together* . . . How right she was. Mr. Barnett and Holly-Heart together? Now, this was some fabulous surprise!

Standing on the other side of the curtain, Miss Hess was explaining to the audience the necessary substitution of characters. The orchestra played a soft interlude as she spoke.

My mind raced ahead to the upcoming scenes. First, I would be introduced to Captain von Trapp at his Austrian villa. Then, several scenes later—the moonlit gazebo scene!

Then it hit me. I knew the perfect way to show Mr. Barnett my true feelings. Thinking ahead, I felt strangely calm. Like this was supposed to be. Fate had brought us together, and now we were here, onstage together, enacting one of the greatest romances of the century.

Slowly, the curtains rose. When the applause died down, I rang the gold-painted doorbell on the prop representing the double doors of the von Trapp villa. The butler, wearing his wig, opened the door to the grand hallway. Maria mistook the butler for the captain, and the scene was under way.

Once again, the incredible rhythm of dialogue and drama began to unfold. It took me back to the day I auditioned, when Mr. Barnett and I had played our parts as if we'd been born to them. Tonight, wearing his dazzling uniform, sparring verbally with me onstage, Andrew Barnett *was* Georg von Trapp. And I, his precious Maria.

♥   ♥   ♥

In the silvery blue moonlight, two lovers sat beneath a gazebo, trees casting dim shadows across their faces. "I can't marry the baroness when I'm in love with someone else," the captain said after a long, endearing look. "Can I, Maria?"

Slowly, coyly, I shook my head.

"I love *you*, Maria," he said, reaching for my chin.

I held my breath as he drew me close . . . closer.

Then, to make the audience think we were kissing, he turned the back of his head toward them, just as Jared and I had practiced. We held the stance while the crowd *ooh*ed softly. And as they did, I gently kissed his cheek.

There. Now he knew.

The orchestra played the introduction of "Something Good" as arms entwined, and eyes filled with tenderness, we sang our beautiful duet. It was surprising how well our voices blended.

At the end of the musical, we bowed repeatedly. Separately, and then together. We were a dynamic hit, Mr. Barnett and I. Quite obvious by the thunderous applause.

Afterward, people rushed onstage, presenting me with flowers. Mom and Uncle Jack were some of the first. Miss Hess was full of compliments, and so was Miss Wannamaker, who held hands with Mr. Ross as she carried on about the performance.

Later, when the audience thinned out a bit, Daddy came up to congratulate me. More flowers. I introduced him to Mr. Barnett, who stood nearby.

"Have you thought of studying drama?" Daddy asked me. "You are a wonderful actress."

"I agree with you," Mr. Barnett said. "Holly seems very comfortable onstage."

"Thank you," I said, blushing. But under all that stage face-goop, who would notice?

"I'll call you from my hotel later," Daddy said, hugging me.

"You made this night extra-special for me, Daddy," I said. "I'll never forget it."

He waved and turned to go. As his figure disappeared into the crowd, I started to cry.

Touching my elbow, Mr. Barnett guided me backstage. "Can I help?" he asked.

I shook my head. "It's a long, sad story."

"Your father certainly loves you." He smiled as I wiped my eyes. "Everyone does."

It was a sweet thing to say. But did he include himself in the comment?

"You'll be leaving soon," I said. "And I'm going to miss you around here."

"I'll miss you, too, Holly," he said kindly. Like a big brother. Then he smiled. "Well," he said, his voice brightening, "if you were just a little older, I'd take you out for a banana split with extra strawberries and whipped cream."

Instantly, his words struck home. "You *knew?*" I covered my mouth. "You knew it was me at the Soda Straw that day?"

"Hey, young nuns with flowing blond hair are few and far between," he said, trying to suppress a grin.

We both burst out laughing. It was a welcome relief—especially after the pressures of seeing Daddy and being alone with Mr. Barnett like this.

"Thanks for keeping quiet about my stupidity," I said, setting my flowers on a chair. "Did Miss Hess know?"

His eyes sparkled with mischief. "If she did, she never let on."

I sighed. "Thank goodness." Then I shot him a sly glance. "Are you and she. . . ?"

He actually blushed, I thought. But he dodged my question. "About that banana split," he said, turning on the charm again. "Where will you be four years from now?"

His friendly teasing made me laugh. "Four years from now? Oh, that's hard to say," I said, playing along. Now that I'd revealed my true feelings, I could relax and just be myself. Besides, I was beginning to see Andrew Barnett for what he really was— a big flirt. Oh, sure, he was a good-looking one. And an older one. But an over-grown Jared just the same.

Mr. Barnett glanced over at Danny and Billy organizing props for tomorrow's show. "There *are* some pretty terrific guys your own age around here, in case you haven't noticed."

Just then Paula came out of the dressing room, carrying a large bouquet of red roses. "These are for you, Holly," she said. "Someone left them during the last scene."

I glanced down at the card. It read: *When the Lord closes a door, somewhere He opens a window. Always, Jared.*

It was a line directly from the musical, where Maria tells Mother Abbess she feels called to work with the von Trapp children instead of staying on at the abbey.

Leaning my face into Jared's roses, I breathed their fragrance deeply. "About those guys my age," I said, smiling up at Mr. Barnett, "maybe you're right."

♥   ♥   ♥

Jared's illness turned out to be a twelve-hour flu, so we performed together the second night. Of course, we were fabulous together, but never would I forget my shining moment—the night I shared the stage with my Mr. Barnett.

The last few days of the semester flew by, and my feelings for our student teacher began to change. For the better. I started to see him for who he was— instead of who I'd daydreamed he could be. A very cool teacher. A good friend. But not future husband material.

Of course, I never knew if he took Miss Hess out again. I decided it was best if I didn't know. Funny how that goes.

Before long, Miss W's wedding day arrived. The faculty and the student body filled the auditorium during the final hour of the school year.

Miss W surprised everyone by wearing a full-length white gown with a six-foot train and a long white veil. Her smile was as sweet as a young bride's.

"I better not be that old when I get married," Andie whispered as "The Wedding March" came over the sound system.

Step by step, the matronly teacher made her way down the long aisle toward Mr. Ross, who was looking mighty spiffy in his long gray tuxedo.

"She's really beautiful." Tears welled up in my eyes.

We turned and watched as she stood beside Mr. Ross at the front. The minister motioned for us to be seated. As he began with "Dearly beloved," I glanced down the row of seats.

My friends, each one, were within hugging distance. Jared and Danny sat directly behind me. Andie and Stan sat on one side of me, and Paula and Billy on the other. Amy-Liz and all the others filled up the seats in the row. Together we witnessed the blending of two lives in holy matrimony.

Next year, Miss W would be known as Mrs. Ross. Not only that, Andie and I would be at the top of the heap—ninth grade. We'd come so far, so fast. Where had the years gone?

Stan, Danny, and the Miller twins were heading off to high school. So many things were changing.

Mr. Barnett was leaving Dressel Hills to graduate

from college, taking his fabulous T-Bird with him . . . and leaving behind a trail of pistachio shells.

Special days, special moments don't last forever. Anyone knows that. Breezes of change blow hard and fast. And before you know it, skinny figures fill out. Kids grow up. Journals burst with top-secret information. Prayers get answered.

I smiled through my tears as the minister pronounced the happy couple husband and wife. We gave Mr. and Mrs. Ross a standing ovation as they walked down the aisle.

♥　♥　♥

Back at my locker, I gathered up my books and papers for the final time. Then I headed toward the front doors. Ahead of me was another fabulous Dressel Hills summer. And behind me—all of eighth grade.

As the glass doors of the school swung shut behind me, I thought of Jared's note. *When the Lord closes a door, somewhere He opens a window.* God was closing a chapter in my life. But by trusting Him, I knew that, in time, a window would fling wide.

And I could hardly wait.

♥ ♥ ♥

Don't miss HOLLY'S HEART #9,
No Guys Pact
Available January 2003!

Holly and her friends are excited about summer camp. What could be better than a week of fun in the mountains of Colorado? But when a little dis-respect from the boys gets them the silent treatment from the girls, they all learn a lesson they'll never forget.

About the Author

Beverly Lewis has always loved the musical *The Sound of Music*. She played its melodies in junior high orchestra in the first-violin section, and she sang the songs with her sister to pass the time while traveling by car to and from college.

A former schoolteacher, Beverly writes from her home near her favorite mountain, Pikes Peak, where the hills are alive with music. Making music at the piano and answering fan mail—both snail mail and email—these are a few of Beverly's favorite things.

If you want to write, she can be contacted through her Web site: *www.BeverlyLewis.com.*

Also by Beverly Lewis

PICTURE BOOKS

Cows in the House   Annika's Secret Wish
Just Like Mama

THE CUL-DE-SAC KIDS
Children's Fiction

The Double Dabble Surprise   Tarantula Toes
The Chicken Pox Panic   Green Gravy
The Crazy Christmas Angel Mystery   Backyard Bandit Mystery
No Grown-ups Allowed   Tree House Trouble
Frog Power   The Creepy Sleep-Over
The Mystery of Case D. Luc   The Great TV Turn-Off
The Stinky Sneakers Mystery   Piggy Party
Pickle Pizza   The Granny Game
Mailbox Mania   Mystery Mutt
The Mudhole Mystery   Big Bad Beans
Fiddlesticks   The Upside-Down Day
The Crabby Cat Caper   The Midnight Mystery

ABRAM'S DAUGHTERS
Adult Fiction

The Covenant

THE HERITAGE OF LANCASTER COUNTY
Adult Fiction

The Shunning   The Confession
The Reckoning

OTHER ADULT FICTION

The Postcard
The Crossroad

October Song

The Redemption of Sarah Cain

Sanctuary*

The Sunroom

www.BeverlyLewis.com

*with David Lewis